"He's blanketed his property with men," Clint said.

They were sitting atop a rise near a cluster of trees, looking down at the three men riding by. It was the fourth such grouping they'd seen in the past half hour.

"Looks like Titus is a little concerned about me," Scarlet commented.

"Concerned . . . or scared."

"How are we going to get to him with all these men around?"

The Gunsmith looked at Scarlet and said, "Maybe we can make him come to us. . . ."

Don't miss any of the lusty, hard-riding action in the
Charter Western series, THE GUNSMITH

And coming next month:
THE GUNSMITH #45: NAVAHO DEVIL

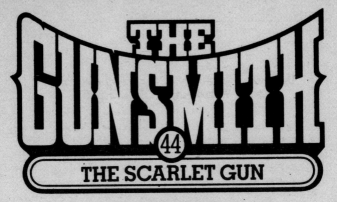

THE GUNSMITH

44

THE SCARLET GUN

J. R. ROBERTS

CHARTER BOOKS, NEW YORK

THE GUNSMITH #44: THE SCARLET GUN

A Charter Book / published by arrangement with
the author

PRINTING HISTORY
Charter edition / September 1985

ISBN: 0-441-30948-8

Charter Books are published by The Berkley Publishing Group,
200 Madison Avenue, New York, New York 10016.
PRINTED IN THE UNITED STATES OF AMERICA

ONE

Sheena O'Shay was twenty-eight years old, tall and slim. She had long, wavy brown hair, wide-set brown eyes, a straight nose that came to a slight point that tipped up—she called it "funny"—a lush, full-lipped mouth . . . and freckles. Only she didn't just have a few freckles, she had freckles that ran over the bridge of her nose and spattered her cheeks, freckles between her pear-shaped, brown tipped breasts and, by golly, freckles across her back.

Clint Adams sat beside her in her bed, staring down at her while she was asleep, taking all of these attributes in. Of course, she didn't consider them all attributes. As well as thinking her nose funny, she said her eyes were *too* widely set apart and her mouth too full, making her look like she was always ready to be kissed.

("And around you," she added in her slight Irish accent, which was just another aspect of her many charms, "I am.")

He argued with her, saying that although he agreed that her eyes *were* too wide apart, her nose *was* unusual, she *did* have a lot of freckles, and her neck *was* too long—("Who said anything about my neck!")—that when you put all of those things together, they made up Sheena O'Shay, and that was fine by him and almost any man in his right mind.

Even asleep she was prettier and more desirable than most of the women he'd met in his life.

She opened her eyes and caught him staring at her.

"How long have you been doing that?"

"What?"

"Staring at me?"

"A long time."

"Why?"

"Because I don't mind it," he said. "It relaxes me."

"Oh, really?" she asked, reaching out and settling her hand between his legs, where it encountered a thickening, hardening stalk of flesh. "You don't feel relaxed."

"Well, it relaxes my mind," he said, reaching for her left breast, "while it excites my body."

She closed her eyes, and as his hand closed over her breast, she tightened her own hold on him.

"Let's not play this time," she said, grinning behind her closed eyes, "let's just do it."

"Are you ready?" he asked. He reached for her with his other hand and found her slick. "Yeah," he said, "you're more than ready."

"So are you," she said, flicking her thumb over the swollen head of his penis.

He moved on top of her, poking at her with his penis and sliding into her with consummate ease.

"Ooh, yes!" she cried as he pierced her deeply, and she wrapped her long legs around him tightly.

He moved his hands beneath her to cup her smooth

buttocks because she had told him often enough that she loved it when he did that, and began to take her in long, even strokes.

"Ah . . ." she moaned, rubbing her hands over his broad back. "That's it, Clint, ooh yes, that's it . . . I love it, squeeze my ass . . . I love it when you squeeze my ass. . . ."

He squeezed her ass and that seemed to set off her orgasm. She bucked beneath him, yanking his orgasm from him, and they went up and down the mountain together.

At breakfast Danny O'Shay said, "When are you leaving, Clint?"

Clint looked at Sheena's twenty-year-old brother across the table and said, "Soon, Danny, soon."

Sheena looked up from her stove and asked, "How soon is soon?"

"You will teach me to shoot before you go, won't you?" Danny asked.

"No, Danny."

"Clint," Sheena asked, "how soon—"

"Why not?" Danny demanded. He stood up—a tall, gangly kid who would be a big man when he filled out some. "I been practicing with my gun, Clint. I'm fast!"

"There's no reason to be fast, Danny," Clint said.

"You're fast!"

"I sometimes wish I wasn't," Clint said, looking at Sheena and seeing the concerned look on her face.

"Well, I'm gonna be!" Danny shouted. "Even without your help, I will be!"

Danny bolted from the room and Clint rose to go after him.

"Let him go, Clint," Sheena said, moving forward

and closing one hand over his left arm. Her eyes moved over his face searchingly and she said, "You're leaving today, aren't you?"

He stared at her and said, "Tomorrow."

"Well," she said, "I knew this day was coming."

"Sheena—"

"It's all right," she said, returning to the stove to preside over the bacon and eggs. "I'm just glad that we met the very first day you came to Hedgemont, and that we didn't waste any time."

Sheena was literally the first person Clint had seen when he first rode into Hedgemont, Colorado, a town he had originally intended simply to pass through—until he found a reason to stay awhile. Now a week had gone by and Clint knew it was time to leave again, time to head on back to Labyrinth, Texas, and some well-needed rest. That town had become something of a haven for the Gunsmith, a place where he could go when he got tired of traveling; where he knew he wouldn't run into any unwanted trouble because he had become known in the town and the people respected him.

"Sheena," he said, putting his hands on her shoulders from behind, "I can't stay in one place—"

"Don't explain," she said, turning into his arms and laying her head on his chest, "just don't try to explain. I understand, I really do. I'm just . . . selfish enough to wish that you could. Go on, now." She pushed him away. "Go sit down and I'll bring you your breakfast."

"What about Danny?"

"He'll eat later."

"No, I mean he was pretty angry—"

"He'll have to get used to the idea that you're

leaving, just like I will,'' she said, putting a plate of food down in front of him. ''We'll just help each other. Don't worry about us, Clint. We'll be fine.''

Clint wondered if Sheena were underplaying her brother's anger. Ever since Clint had arrived in town and Danny O'Shay had found out who he was, the kid had been pestering him to teach him how to use a gun the proper way. From what Clint had heard, the boy did have some natural speed and a hankering to be a gun-fighter. No matter how many times he tried to tell the kid that the life of a gunfighter was not glamorous or exciting, the boy—the young *man*—refused to listen, and just as steadfastly, Clint refused to tutor him with a gun.

He hoped he'd get a chance to talk to Danny again before he left Hedgemont.

The next morning Sheena O'Shay accompanied Clint Adams to the Hedgemont livery stable and watched while he prepared his team and rig for travel and saw to his huge black gelding, Duke. She watched in silence because she knew there was nothing she could say that would make this man stay with her. She was sure that many women had tried before, and failed.

When Clint was finally ready to leave Hedgemont, Sheena saw him off, but Danny O'Shay was nowhere to be found, and the Gunsmith still had not had the opportunity to talk to him again.

''I'm sorry he didn't come to say good-bye,'' Clint said to Sheena.

She kissed him tenderly and watched as he climbed aboard his rig.

''He'll be sorry he didn't say good-bye too,'' Sheena said, and as Clint rode away, she added to herself, "I'm kind of sorry I did."

Sheena O'Shay had been looking for a man all her life, and now that she had found him, he was riding out of her life and there was nothing she could do about it.

TWO

In another part of the country a woman as beautiful—possibly even more beautiful than Sheena O'Shay— was also looking for a man. In fact, she was looking for more than one man, but she had something totally different in mind for them when she found them.

Her name was Scarlet.

Well, actually her name wasn't Scarlet, but she called herself Scarlet. Her real name was part of her past, most of which she had put behind her, forgotten.

All except her thirst for revenge. That was deeply rooted in her past, and it was something she clung to very tightly because it was all that meant anything to her.

Scarlet was a tall, full-bodied redhead who, at sixteen, was beautiful enough to make a man's hands itch and his teeth ache. As she grew older, she grew even more beautiful, and now, at the age of twenty-three, she could not only use her gun with deadly accuracy but had also learned to use her beauty as a deadly weapon—against men!

Scarlet's vengeance was meant for five men in particular but it often lent itself to other men who crossed her path—men who reminded her of those five who had destroyed her family and snatched her innocence from her before she could give it to a man out of love.

Her present path was moving inexorably toward that of the Gunsmith. It remained to be seen whether Clint Adams would fall prey to the woman who called herself Scarlet—and, if so, in what way.

THREE

Labyrinth, Texas.

If Clint Adams had a home, this was it—and yet he declined to refer to it as that. This was his place, his haven, and even so he rarely spent more than a couple of weeks at a time here. Still, he had an account in the Labyrinth Bank and he had at least one good friend— Rick Hartman of the saloon Rick's Place.

It was always very odd to the Gunsmith that he felt comfortable in this town, since this was where he'd been when he first heard of his friend Bill Hickok's death—or murder! He'd gone a little crazy then and maybe that was why he felt at ease here. The town, and Rick Hartman in particular, had seen him at his worst, and still they accepted him.

He stayed away from the women in Labyrinth as a rule, not wanting to form any attachments here which would interfere with his coming here to rest . . . from everything. There was a woman here for a while that he had met elsewhere—Mary Randall*—but she had

*The Gunsmith #39: The El Paso Salt War.
 The Gunsmith #41: Hell With a Pistol.

since moved on, which was just as well. It would have been easy to get used to having her around.

Poker was the form of relaxation Clint preferred to indulge in while staying in Labyrinth, and Rick's Place was where he usually played. To keep on friendly terms, he played for small stakes in a regular game. He was the only non-regular allowed in the game, as they allowed that he was more of a semi-regular, playing whenever he was in town.

"How are you doing?" Rick Hartman asked, coming alongside Clint as he was playing a pat hand.

"Watch," Clint said.

He had been dealt a low straight which stood up against the liveryman's three of a kind.

"Cleaning these boys out?"

"Do us a favor, Rick," Maxwell, the liveryman, said, "take him away from here for a while so someone else can have a chance to win."

"I think I'll do just that," Rick said, slapping the Gunsmith on the back. "Why don't you come to my office and have a drink with me, Clint?"

"Are you buying?"

"Don't be funny," Rick said. "I always buy in my own office—in fact, in my own saloon, as far as you're concerned. Come on, I want to talk to you."

Clint saw that his friend had something on his mind and said, "All right, then. You boys will have to struggle along without me for a while."

"Praise be," the liveryman said, and the others laughed as Clint collected his money and followed Rick Hartman to his office.

"What's on your mind, Rick?" Clint asked, once they were comfortably seated with a brandy each.

Rick grinned. "Well, for one thing that new girl of mine," he said, referring to a young lady he'd just hired to work the saloon. "Have you seen her?"

"I'm not blind, Rick."

She was a tall, young brunette, slim but nicely put together—*very* nicely put together, with a full-breasted figure—in spite of her overall slimness, which was shown to good advantage by the low-cut gowns she wore while working. He knew her name was Emma but didn't know her last name.

Rick swirled the brandy in his snifter. "But that's not what I wanted to tell you about." He stared at Clint, then sighed and took something from his inner jacket pocket. "You got a telegram today."

"When?"

"Just a little while ago."

"You screening my mail now?"

"You only just got here," Rick said, handing him the telegram.

Clint read it and was surprised to find that it was from Sheena O'Shay, until he remembered telling her about Labyrinth.

"What's the problem?" Rick asked, reading the expression on his friend's face.

"A lady I knew for a while seems to have a problem," Clint said, folding the telegram.

"And she wants you to fix it?"

Clint stared at the far wall and said, "I probably could have prevented the problem if I'd known—"

"And how could you know about a problem that arose after you left?"

"I should have seen it coming."

Clint tossed the telegram on the desk and Rick interpreted that as permission to read it:

DANNY HAS KILLED A MAN AND HAS RUN OFF TO BE A GUNFIGHTER. PLEASE FIND HIM.

"Short and to the point," Rick said, dropping the telegram onto the desk. "Another youngster who fancies himself a fast gun, right?"

"That's right. He kept asking me to teach him how to use a gun properly and I kept putting him off."

"Well, judging from this, he's learned to use one fairly well on his own."

"I guess."

"Are you going?"

"I'll have to find him," Clint said, standing up. "I could have kept this from happening, Rick. Maybe I can keep him from ending up like . . . "

"Like that boy who was claiming to be your son?" Rick finished.*

"Yeah," Clint said. "Maybe I can keep him from getting himself killed."

"He's not your responsibility, Clint."

"Responsibility is something you take on yourself, Rick," Clint said, heading for the door. "That's just what I'm doing."

---

*The Gunsmith #41: Hell with a Pistol.

FOUR

Clint sent and received a series of telegrams over the next few days, and the news he received back—from Sheena, and from friends and contacts around the country—was very discouraging.

Danny O'Shay had not gotten in touch with his sister since leaving, and since she had sent Clint the telegram, he'd killed another man and bragged about it. All in all he'd been gone two weeks and killed two men.

That was enough to build a reputation on—a reputation the boy didn't deserve. A reputation that would surely get Danny O'Shay killed.

Clint couldn't help but think that if he had taken more time with the boy in Hedgemont, none of this would have happened. Two men would still be alive, and Danny O'Shay would still be more of a boy and not a killer.

When Clint had finally gathered enough information from his exchange of telegrams to be able to pick up

Danny O'Shay's trail, he was ready to leave Labyrinth.

"So where will you be starting?" Rick asked Clint as he saddled Duke. "Back in Colorado?"

"No, I've been able to trace his trail. I'm going to pick it up in Wyoming and follow it from there."

"A clear trail, do you think?"

"Is that a slur on my tracking abilities?"

Rick laughed and asked, "What tracking abilities?"

"You might have a point there," Clint said, "but I think there'll be a clear enough trail even for me to follow."

Clint fell silent then and Rick asked, "What's worrying you now?"

"I'm afraid when I pick up his trail, it will end up being a trail of bodies."

"He's been lucky up to now."

"Yes, lucky," Clint said, pulling the cinch tight on Duke's saddle, "and he always had some natural speed, but when he comes up against an experienced gun—"

"You'll just have to get to him first," Rick said, trying to assure his friend. "You will."

"I hope so, Rick," Clint said. "I really hope so."

Clint picked up Danny O'Shay's trail in a Wyoming town called Dutch Neck.

"Yep, he was here," Sheriff Pat Brutto said. They were in the sheriff's office. Clint had asked the lawman if he had seen Danny O'Shay and went on to describe the boy.

"There ain't no need to describe him, either," Brutto continued. "He made damn sure that everyone knew who he was after he shot down poor Fred Travers."

"In a fair fight?"

The lawman snorted and said, "If you could call it a fair fight."

"What do you mean?"

"Fred Travers was no gunman," Brutto said in disgust. "He was a farmer—and a family man! He got into an argument with your Danny O'Shay—an argument started by O'Shay, I could add—and it ended up out in the street. If your boy—"

"He's not my boy," Clint interrupted, and his vehemence surprised even himself.

"All right," Brutto said. "If this O'Shay is building a rep on men like Fred Travers, then you can be sure it's a hollow one."

"I suppose it is," Clint said. "Tell me, Sheriff. Did you try to arrest O'Shay?"

"For what?" Brutto said, scowling. "It *looked* like a fair fight, Adams. What could I do? Oh, I talked to him, but he was like most youngsters these days. He showed me no more respect than he showed Fred Travers. I advised him to leave town and he did, making sure to tell me that he had intended to leave anyway. Why are you looking for him?"

"I'm a friend . . . of his family."

"Well, by the time you catch up to him he may get into an argument with the wrong man and solve your problem for you," Brutto observed. "I can't say I'd be real sorry if that happened."

Clint allowed the remark to pass unacknowledged and said, "I appreciate your help, Sheriff Brutto."

"Sure," Brutto said. As Clint started for the door, he called out, "Adams!"

"Yeah?"

"Talking about reps," the lawman said, standing up

in order to make his meaning plain, "how long do you intend to stay in town—not that I object, mind you. I'm just . . . the curious type." The sheriff hitched up his gunbelt, as if attempting to assert himself, but that was difficult to do when you were only five-feet-four-inches tall.

"Just long enough to get a meal and night in a bed under my belt, Sheriff," Clint said without hesitation. "You've got nothing to worry about. I won't be here long enough for anyone to even notice me."

"Thanks," Brutto said, and he seemed to mean it. "I appreciate that."

"Sure."

The Gunsmith had his meal and his night's sleep, and for once his intention to stay out of trouble held up. Early the next morning he started for the next town under the watchful eye of Sheriff Brutto.

How many bodies, he thought, am I going to have to climb over to find you, Danny?

At that moment, Danny O'Shay was leaving a town in Nevada called Averyville and heading for the next town, Pleasant Point. He had four kills under his belt now and was feeling very cocky about himself. Cocky enough to reply to a call for a gunfighter by a rancher in that town who had need of a fast gun.

A need that Danny O'Shay intended to fill.

Somewhere in between Clint Adams and Danny O'Shay rode the woman called Scarlet.

She was not following Danny O'Shay's trail but a trail left by one of the five men she had been seeking for years. Two of those five men were already dead, and this one would be the third. She wouldn't rest until she had found and killed all five.

For an entirely different reason, she was heading straight for Pleasant Point, Nevada. She would find cocky young Danny O'Shay there ahead of her, and coming not long after—the Gunsmith.

They were all on a collision course which would come together in Pleasant Point.

FIVE

When Danny O'Shay arrived in Pleasant Point he knew only that a ranch named Titus needed a gunman.

There was much he didn't know.

He didn't know that John Titus was one of the biggest ranchers in Nevada, a man with much wealth and even more political aspirations; he didn't know that Titus wanted a gunman he could use and then throw to the wolves when the job was done; and he didn't know that John Titus was the third man on Scarlet's list.

He also didn't know where the Titus ranch was located, but that problem was solved simply by asking someone in town. Everyone in Pleasant Point knew John Titus and where he lived, and most of the people respected him and were prepared to support any political move he made.

There were only a few who knew John Titus for what he really was, and they were the reason Titus needed a gunman.

Danny O'Shay was applying for the job.

"There's a man outside to see you, Boss," Frank Valin told John Titus. Valin was Titus's foreman and had known him a long time, but even he was required to knock before entering Titus's private office.

"A man? Is he here for the job?"

"Well," Valin, a man in his late thirties, replied with a smirk, "I guess I stretched the truth when I said he was a man. He's a kid, Boss."

"How old?"

Valin shrugged and said, "Ah, nineteen, twenty, something like that."

"Is he wearing a gun?"

"Sure," Valin replied in a tone that plainly said—everyone wears a gun.

"How's he wear it?"

Valin frowned and said, "On his hip—"

"No, I mean does he wear it like he can use it?" Titus said impatiently.

"I guess," Valin said, shrugging.

"All right, Frank," Titus said, realizing that he'd have to judge for himself, "bring him in."

Valin left the office to fetch the young man and Titus sat back in his chair to wait, hoping this would be someone he could use.

John Titus was a white-haired man in his late forties who thought that his prematurely white hair would be a political asset. It gave him a more dignified look, and that was important in political life. He was also tall, slim, and not unattractive, all of which, he thought, combined with his cleverness, would bring him the success he sought.

First, though, he had to rid himself of a few thorns in his side.

The greatest danger seemed to come from another big rancher in the area, Victor Barrow. Titus knew that Barrow had detectives looking into his past, and there was one incident he could not afford to have unearthed. He couldn't kill the detectives, though, because there were plenty of men to replace them. What he had to do was do away with the man paying them. Once the money stopped coming, they'd stop digging.

Barrow had two friends who shared his suspicions about Titus. One was the banker, George Garvin, and the other the hotel owner, an elderly man named Dave Quinn.

Titus thought Quinn would be easy to kill. He was old and his death could be made to look accidental. And Garvin might not have to be killed. When Barrow was gone, Garvin probably wouldn't be a problem, but that remained to be seen.

Titus needed a gunman to throw *at* Barrow, and then throw *to* the townspeople, and maybe a younger man would be easier to . . . control.

When Valin returned with the young man, Titus had just about decided that the man's age worked in his favor. Now all that remained was to be convinced that the man had some talent with a gun.

That was really all he needed to have—*some* talent. There were no gunmen in Barrow's employ to worry about.

"This is Danny O'Shay, Boss," Valin said. "O'Shay, this is Mr. Titus."

"Glad to meet you, Mr. Titus," O'Shay said, grinning. Valin had been right, Titus observed. O'Shay couldn't have been more than twenty.

"You heard I was . . . looking for someone to do a job for me?"

"I heard you were looking for a gun," O'Shay said with a smirk.

"Where did you hear that?"

"Averyville, just south of here."

"Word's getting around," Titus said, looking at Valin.

"You said to spread it—" Valin began, but Titus silenced him with a glance.

"I don't think you'll have to spread the word anymore, Mr. Titus," Danny O'Shay said. "I'm the man you need."

"What qualification can you offer?" Titus asked. "Should I know your name?"

O'Shay shrugged and said, "I killed a man in Dewey, Nevada, a week ago. You might have heard about that."

"I think I did," Titus lied. He'd heard nothing about a gunfight in Dewey or any other Nevada town in the past week. "How fast are you, O'Shay?"

O'Shay drew his gun in response and said, "I'm fast, Mr. Titus."

Indeed, Titus agreed that the boy was swift when it came to producing his gun, but could he hit what he aimed at?

"Where did you learn how to use a gun, O'Shay?"

"I learned from the best, Mr. Titus," O'Shay said without hesitation. He had already decided what his answer to that question would be. "I learned from Clint Adams, the Gunsmith himself."

Titus was impressed—if it was true.

"All right, O'Shay," he said, clasping his hands in

front of him. "I'm going to give you a try. Frank, show Mr. O'Shay to the bunkhouse."

"I'm gonna bunk with the hands?" O'Shay asked, obviously experiencing some disappointment.

"Don't worry, O'Shay," Titus said. "You'll be paid enough to make up for not having your own quarters. In fact, if you work out, it might just be that you'll get your own place—in time."

"All right, Mr. Titus," O'Shay said, his youthful cockiness in full evidence. "I'll give *you* a try."

Titus stiffened, but then relaxed and said, "We'll try each other out, O'Shay. I'm sure we'll both be satisfied."

"Thanks, Mr. Titus."

The boy was tall, eager, didn't seem overly bright, and had certainly drawn his gun with more speed than anyone Barrow had on his spread, Titus thought as Valin led O'Shay out of the room.

O'Shay might just work out, Titus conceded.

They'd find out soon enough.

SIX

Clint Adams had heard about the gunfight that had taken place in Dewey, Nevada, and arrived there a couple of weeks after it happened. Although the word had not spread far and wide—the way it might have had it been between two name gunmen—it had spread to certain parts of Nevada, and upon entering Nevada Clint had heard about it in the first town he stopped in. He immediately set out for Dewey, bypassing towns in between.

Consequently, he and Duke were somewhat the worse for wear when they rode into Dewey. Clint took care of the necessities for himself and Duke before seeking out the local sheriff.

"It was kind of a shock to all of us," Sheriff Tom Clayton admitted. Clayton was a portly man in his forties who looked as if he spent more time behind his desk than on the streets.

"Why is that?"

"Well, Lanny Hunt was a local celebrity here in Dewey, Mr. Adams." Clayton had recognized the Gunsmith's name as soon as Clint introduced himself

25

and had been treating him with the utmost respect ever since. "I guess you could say he was the house gun."

"You're a gambler, Sheriff?" Clint asked. Referring to anyone, or anything, as the "house" indicated a propensity for gambling. Clint, a gambler himself, had used the term more than once.

"Well, I've played a card now and then, why?"

"Never mind. You're saying that this Lanny Hunt was the town's fast gun and O'Shay took him?"

The sheriff pursed his lips, pushed out some air, and said, "Easy."

Clint frowned. Was O'Shay growing more proficient with every man he killed? If that was the case then the kid was also going to grow more cocky. Sooner or later he was going to force the hand of a better man, and that would be the end of it.

Unless Clint could get there first.

"Did you run him out of town?"

"I'd like to say I did," the lawman said, "but he said he was leaving anyway. How many does that make for him?"

"Why do you ask?"

"He struck me as a lad trying real hard to build himself a rep."

That surprised Clint. The sheriff had not struck him as a particularly observant man, and he was beginning to think that he had underestimated him.

"You're right," Clint said, "and by my count this makes four."

"I ain't even fired my gun at that many people in my life," Clayton said, shaking his head. "Not that I don't do my job, but I find other ways of doing it than with my gun. I'm not real good with a gun, Adams, but then you was a lawman. You know that different men are good at different things.''

"I know that,'' Clint said. He rose, feeling as if he should apologize to the man for judging him so quickly and wrongly.

"Can you tell me which way he was headed, Sheriff?'' he asked.

"Sure, toward Averyville—''

"Thanks.''

"—but I don't think he'll stay there.''

"Why do you say that?''

"Heard a rumor, is all.''

"What kind of rumor?''

"The kind not too many people put stock in,'' Clayton said, ''but this lad might.''

"Why?''

"We got us a big man in Nevada, Mr. Adams. John Titus. Ever heard of him?''

"Can't say I have.''

"You will if he has his way. Gonna be a big man in politics.''

"Good for him. What's this got to do with Danny O'Shay?''

"Well, I heard tell that Mr. Titus was looking to hire himself a gun. Seems to me a fella like this O'Shay would jump at a chance like that.''

"Seems to me you might be right,'' Clint said. "Where would this fellow Titus live?''

"Pleasant Point,'' Clayton said. ''Just head right on past Averyville and you can't miss it. Take you a couple of days hard ride.''

"I'll have to rest my horse a day before I ride him that hard,'' Clint said, more to himself than to the lawman.

"Well, you're welcome to stay in Dewey as long as you like."

"I am?" Clint asked, surprised. Not many lawmen welcomed him, or men like him, in their towns for more than a day.

"Sure," Clayton said. "With Lanny Hunt dead ain't nobody in town likely to try you out."

"Are you saying that this Hunt fellow pushed the fight with O'Shay?"

"Well, he sure didn't back away from it, that's for sure. Let's just say those young fellas eyed each other right off and there was no stopping them after that."

"No," Clint said, "there never is. Thanks for your hospitality, Sheriff, but I don't think I'll be taking advantage of it for more than a day."

"Ride hard to get here, did you?"

"I did."

"And you figure to push your horse after only a day's rest?"

"I do."

Clayton shook his head and said, "That must be some kind of horse you got."

Clint nodded, said, "He is," and left.

SEVEN

During Clint's one day in Dewey, Danny O'Shay had his baptism of fire.

"Who do you want dead?" he asked John Titus during a meeting in Titus's office.

Titus stared at the young man and then said, "Oh, anyone, as long as they work for Victor Barrow."

"Really?" O'Shay asked, his eyes lighting up like a kid in a candy store who has just been told he can have anything he wants.

"Really," Titus said, then added, "but there are other conditions."

"What's that?" O'Shay asked, frowning.

It took Titus a moment to realize that Danny O'Shay didn't know what the word condition meant. "That means that there's one other thing I want you to make sure of."

"What?"

"I want it to be a fair fight," Titus said. "I want everyone to know who you are, after you kill . . . whoever . . . and I don't want anyone to know that you work for me. Do you understand?"

29

"Yes, sir."

"It's got to look good, Danny," Titus went on. "All right?"

"Sure," O'Shay said, "but I still get paid, right?"

"Of course."

"That's great, Mr. Titus," O'Shay said. "When do I do this?"

"Today."

"Now?"

"Fine," Titus said. "Go to town, Danny. Make me proud." That last remark amused Titus, since he'd never had a son he could say it to. "Make me proud."

After Frank Valin saw Danny O'Shay leave the house, mount up, and ride toward town, he went into Titus's office.

"Boss?" he said, knocking and entering.

"Frank, did he leave?"

"Yes."

"Take two men and go to town," Titus said. "Watch him, watch him closely, Frank. Watch what he does. You know what I want. If it looks like it's going to go wrong, kill him."

"Yes, sir."

"Kill him quick, Frank," Titus went on, as if instructing a child. "I don't want this getting back to me. Do you understand?"

"Yes, sir."

It never occurred to Frank Valin to wonder what would happen to him after he killed Danny O'Shay.

Danny O'Shay took his time making his choice.

He found a group of four Barrow hands in the

saloon—he checked with the bartender to make sure—and then, over a beer at a corner table, he watched them and carefully made his choice.

One man was too old; one wore his gun as if he wouldn't have been able to find it if his life depended on it; a third was too fat—his girth would have made it impossible for him to reach his gun.

Remembering what John Titus had said about it having to look fair, Danny O'Shay made his choice. The fourth man was tall, slim, in his thirties, and looked as if he could handle himself. He also had a quality, an air about him, that made Danny O'Shay sure he would be easy to push into a fight.

Danny got up and went to do what he'd become very good at doing—instigating a confrontation. Although he had absolutely no knowledge of psychology—and indeed would not have known the meaning of the word had he ever heard it—he had learned that the best way to make a man fight was to challenge his pride.

And he had become very good at picking the prideful man out of a bunch.

Clint Adams was leaving Dewey as the sheriff of Pleasant Point was releasing Danny O'Shay from custody. Witnesses stated that, after an altercation in the saloon, the dead man, Steve Dodd, actually demanded that O'Shay step out into the street.

"I don't know you, O'Shay," Sheriff Bill Resnick said, "but I'd like you to leave town . . . today."

"Are you telling me to?"

"I'm telling you what I'd like you to do," Resnick, a bulky man in his fifties, said.

"I can't leave."

"Why not?"

O'Shay hesitated, then said, "I like it here."

"I can't make you leave, son," Resnick said, "but I could make you wish you had."

O'Shay stood up and said, "Thanks very much, Sheriff."

As he left the office the sheriff shook his head and said, "Why me?"

Cal Franklin and Zeke Perry kept their eyes on Frank Valin as O'Shay left the sheriff's office.

"Frank?" Perry asked.

"Looks all right to me, boys," Valin said. They watched as O'Shay mounted up and rode out of town in the direction of the Titus ranch.

"You fellas go on back to the ranch. Tell the boss I'll be there soon."

When Valin returned to the ranch he saw O'Shay leaning against the livery stable, talking to two of the hands. The foreman went directly into the house and knocked on John Titus's office door.

"Boss?"

"How did it go?"

"Fine," Valin said. "I talked to the sheriff—just out of curiosity—and he said there was nothing he could do. It was a fair fight."

Titus nodded and said, "All right."

"What do we do now?"

"We'll wait a while and see what Barrow does."

Valin nodded then, turned to leave, then turned back and said, "Boss?"

"Yes?"

"Uh, don't you want to know who O'Shay killed?"

Titus waved the man away and said, "That's not important."

EIGHT

The woman called Scarlet rode into Dewey an hour after Danny O'Shay rode out. She pulled her horse up in front of the sheriff's office, tethered the animal, and entered.

"Sheriff?"

Resnick looked up briefly, dropped his eyes back to his desk, then suddenly lifted them again.

"Uh—" he said.

"Are you the sheriff?"

He nodded, speechless. He had never seen a woman as beautiful as this one. He didn't even notice that she wore her gun as if she knew how to use it.

"I'm looking for a man named Titus, Sheriff," she announced.

"Uh, there's a John Titus—"

"That's him. Does he live in town?"

"No," the sheriff said, then paused to moisten his lips. "Uh, he has a ranch . . . outside of town."

"Which way?"

"North."

35

"Thank you."

She turned to leave and the sheriff called out desperately, "Wait!"

"Yes?"

What, he thought, could he say to her that would make her stay?

"Uh, what do you want with Mr. Titus?"

She smiled at him—he had never seen anyone so beautiful in his life—mumbled something and left. It wasn't until a few minutes later that he realized what she had said.

"I'm going to kill him."

After the spell cast by the red-haired woman passed and the sheriff realized the importance of what she'd said, he left his office to find someone who worked at the Titus ranch—anyone. He felt Titus should know about it, even if she was just a woman.

The word eventually reached Frank Valin, who decided to pass it on to his boss, even though he thought the woman was either kidding or crazy.

"Boss?"

Titus looked up from his desk and said, "I told you, Frank, I don't care who he killed."

"No, that's not it, Boss."

"What, then?"

"I just heard something from town that I thought you should know about, even though it's probably silly."

"What is it?"

"I probably shouldn't even bother you with it."

"What is it?"

"Uh, Boss, maybe I should just forget—"

"Valin!"

"A woman rode into town today and told the sheriff she was looking for you."

"So?"

"He asked her what she wanted you for."

"That's what I pay him for, isn't it?"

"She said—"

"Valin."

"Well, Boss, she said she was going to kill you."

Valin stared at Titus, whose face revealed nothing of the turmoil he was experiencing inside.

Had she finally come? he wondered. "What did this woman look like?" he asked, very deliberately.

"The sheriff said she was very beautiful."

"What did she look like!"

"Tall, red hair—"

"Was she wearing a gun?"

"Yes."

"Get out!"

"Boss—"

"Wait," Titus said, changing his mind. "I want you to go to town and send a telegram."

"To who?"

Titus wrote very quickly on a piece of paper, then handed it to Valin.

The foreman read it, then looked at Titus and said, "Boss, we already have a hired gun."

"O'Shay won't be able to handle this," Titus said. "I need someone who's more than just a throwaway gun. Just send it."

Valin started for the door, but his curiosity got the better of him and he turned back again.

"Boss, this woman—"

"Get out, Valin," Titus snapped, "and send that telegram."

Valin left with a puzzled look on his face. As soon as the door closed behind him, John Titus's gray head fell into his hands.

Could this be the same girl, a woman now, looking for revenge? he wondered. He had heard stories about Rogers and Spillner, two men who had been with him back then, two men who had since been killed—by a woman with red hair, it was said.

The girl, all those years ago—she'd had red hair, and she had been the only one left alive. It happened so long ago. In fact, it was that very part of his past that he was trying to keep Barrow's detectives from finding—

—and now it had found him!

After leaving the sheriff's office, Scarlet took her horse to the livery then registered at the hotel simply as *Scarlet*, captivating the hotel clerk as she had the sheriff.

The sheriff, later checking the register to find out the woman's name, simply shrugged when he saw that she had signed in as *Scarlet*, and left the hotel to send John Titus that piece of information.

Scarlet dropped her saddlebags on the bed in her room, then dropped her shapely butt right next to them. She was tired and that frightened her. So far, she had only killed two of the five men she had been seeking for six years, and she was tired. She knew she couldn't afford that, especially when she was this close to taking care of number three.

Her plan now was simply to wait a day or two and see what happened. She knew that the man calling

himself "John Titus" would hear that she was in town.
Her visit to the sheriff just now assured that, which had
been her intent. She knew very well that John Titus was
a big man in Pleasant Point, and that word would get to
him that she was in town looking for him.

The first move was going to be his.

The last move would be hers!

NINE

The next day a move was made in error, and it almost cost a few lives. . . .

Scarlet was having breakfast in the hotel dining room when three men entered and took a table. Unbeknownst to her at the time, the three were from the Titus ranch and they had heard talk about a red-haired woman in town who was looking for their boss, making threats.

"Hey, who does that look like?" one of the men asked the other two. His name was Johnson.

A second man, Miller, said, "I don't know who she is, but I'll tell you what she looks like."

The third man, Wallace, said, "What?"

"Somebody I'd like to know," Miller said.

"No, don't you remember?" Johnson said, annoyed at both of them. "The red-haired gal who was making threats against Mr. Titus."

"That's her?" Wallace asked.

"How many red-haired gals do you think are in town that look like that?" Miller asked.

"We got to do something," Johnson said.

"I know what I'd like to do to her," Miller said, keeping his eyes on the woman while she ate her breakfast.

Wallace laughed, but Johnson said, "I'm serious, dammit."

"Johnson, how serious could she be about killing Titus?" Miller asked. "She could probably kill him in bed—what a way to die—but I don't think that's what she'd have in mind."

"Whatever she's got in mind," Johnson argued, "it would be a feather in our caps to get rid of her."

"Get rid of her?" Miller said. "Are you crazy, man. I want that filly to stick around—"

"You wanna be a cowpuncher all your life, Miller?" Johnson asked, standing up. "I don't."

Johnson left them at the table and walked toward the woman. Miller and Wallace exchanged glances, then shrugged and followed.

As they reached their friend's side, they heard him say, "I want to talk to you, lady."

The redhead looked up at them. Miller groaned inside as he saw her clear, green eyes and watched her lick egg yolk off her lower lip, which caused his pants to tighten suddenly in the groin.

"Can I help you?"

"You sure can," Johnson said. "You can tell us what you mean by threatening our boss."

"Your boss?" the woman said, blinking. "I don't think I understand—"

"You understand, all right," Johnson said. "You

told the sheriff you were here to kill John Titus.''

"Titus is your boss?"

"That's right," Wallace blustered, not wanting to be left out now. "We're Titus's hands."

"That's right," Miller chimed in, but he only did it so the woman would look at him with her green eyes.

"I see," she said. "Did he send you to harass me?"

"To do what—" Wallace started.

"He didn't send us," Johnson said, cutting him off. "We're here on our own."

"What can I do for you?" she asked again.

"Why don't you stand up, walk out of here, and leave town?" Johnson asked.

"Well," she said, looking him in the eye, "one reason would be because I haven't finished my breakfast."

"I can help you with that—" Johnson started, and reached for her plate.

She had been eating steak and eggs and consequently had a steak knife in her hand—a sharp steak knife. She demonstrated its sharpness by driving it through the back of Johnson's right hand, pinning him to the wooden table.

"Wha—" he said, too shocked to even yell. In point of fact the pain was sort of dull, not the kind to produce a scream at all, and he merely gaped at his trapped hand, as did his two partners.

"What did you do?" Wallace finally managed to blurt out.

"I'm sorry," she said, "but I'm paying for this breakfast and I had the feeling that your friend was going to toss it on the floor."

"But look what you did—"

"Oh, this?" she asked, and pulled the knife out.

Now Johnson screamed, burying his hand beneath his left armpit in an attempt to ward off the pain.

"I'll kill you!" he shouted. He started to grab for his gun, but he was right-handed and as he flexed the fingers of that hand he screamed in pain again.

Scarlet stood up, just in case the other two men went for their guns.

"You men want to try?" she asked. "I hate killing before I've finished my breakfast, but I've done it before. It's your choice if I do it again."

The tableau these four presented was the center of attraction at that moment, the other people in the room waiting to see what the men would decide.

The redheaded woman's confidence, plus the shocking thing she had done with the steak knife, persuaded the Titus hands to back off a bit.

"Get your friend to a doctor," she advised them, "before he gets an infection. I don't know how clean the hotel keeps its knives."

Johnson looked as if he wanted to say something but he was too busy whimpering to try. The other two men took hold of him and walked him out of the dining room.

To the surprise of everyone in the room, the woman sat down and appeared to be ready to finish her breakfast when she stopped abruptly and called for a waiter.

"Uh, can I h-help you, Miss?" the waiter asked, nervously eyeing the steak knife in her hand.

"Yes," she said. "I need another knife, please. I got this one dirty."

"Of c-course," the waiter said. He simply reached

over to an empty table, plucked a clean knife from it, and handed it to her.

"Thank you," she said, then proceeded to finish her breakfast.

"Who the fuck's idea was that?" John Titus demanded of Frank Valin.

"Well, Mr. Titus," Valin said, backing away from his employer's tone, "the boys just thought they'd be doing you a favor—"

"Fire them!"

"What?"

"Fire them!"

"But, Boss, they're good boys," Valin argued, "and Johnson's hand—"

"Get rid of them, Valin," Titus said, leaning his elbows on his desk, "or I'll get rid of you. The choice is yours, and I suspect it will be an easy one."

"Yes, sir," Valin said without hesitation. "I'll fire them."

"Well, Missy," Sheriff Bill Resnick said, "it appears you had some fun this morning."

"Fun?" Scarlet asked, raising one delicate eyebrow over one lovely green eye. She was in the sheriff's office at his request, a request he had made in person at the hotel, which she had complied with immediately. "I don't think I follow you, Sheriff."

"Sure you do," Resnick said. This time he was determined not to be intimidated by her beauty. "Seems you put a knife through the hand of one of John Titus's men—"

"Oh, that," she said, folding her arms beneath her

generous breasts. The move nearly undermined Resnick's resolve, but he hung on tenaciously.

"Yes, that," he said.

"That wasn't fun, Sheriff," she said. "Those men were harassing me and I put a stop to it."

"You picked a hell of a way to do it, I don't mind telling you."

"Do you really think so?"

"Well, I wasn't there, but—"

"That's right, Sheriff, you weren't there," Scarlet said, nodding. "Let me tell you, I could just as well have killed that man—or all three."

"Now, Missy—"

"Sheriff," she said, elevating her gaze to the ceiling, "I'd appreciate it a whole lot if you stopped calling me Missy. I don't like it."

Resnick frowned and then reminded himself that this was *his* office, by golly, and he would be the one to make demands.

"All right, *Miss*," he said. "I would appreciate it if you would do one of two things."

"And what would that be?"

"Either leave my town," Resnick said, "or keep clear of trouble—and John Titus."

"Well, Sheriff," she said, "that's one of the few times in my life that someone has given me two choices—neither of which I have any intention of taking."

"What?"

"You want me out of town?" she asked.

"Yes!" he said, sticking his jaw out belligerently.

"Put me out!"

"What?"

"You heard me," Scarlet said, feeling reasonably sure that Resnick was working for Titus. "Either put me out or stop making noises like a lawman."

"Now wait just a—" the sheriff began, but at that point Scarlet turned on her heels and walked out of the office, leaving Sheriff Bill Resnick standing there with his mouth open and his heart pounding wildly.

TEN

When Clint Adams rode into Pleasant Point, it looked like just that—a pleasant point to be riding into. He knew it wasn't, however, because he could feel the tension in the air. His ability to do that had not been laid aside with the badge he'd worn for so long. Those instincts lived on forever, long after the tin star had rusted away, and they would continue to do so.

He was undecided at first whether to go directly to the sheriff's office or do the livery-hotel run first. He finally decided to see the local law. If O'Shay had not stopped in Pleasant Point then there would be no point in his stopping there either. If, on the other hand, the boy *was* in town, he could register at the hotel and plan his next move.

He left Duke standing untethered outside the sheriff's office and entered without knocking.

"Excuse me, Sheriff?"

A bulky man wearing a tin star looked up from his desk and said, "Yeah?"

"You're the sheriff?"

The man's face made obvious the fact that he wished

49

he wasn't—things had probably been bad lately—but finally he said, "Yeah, that's me, Sheriff Resnick. What can I do for you, stranger?" Resnick ran his hands over his face.

"My name is Clint Adams."

The sheriff's hands dropped to the desk as he stared in awe at the Gunsmith.

"I resign."

"Well, before you do that," Clint said, approaching the desk, "we have some business."

"W-what business?"

"I'm looking for a man."

The sheriff closed his eyes tightly and asked, "What man?"

"His name is O'Shay, Danny O'Shay," Clint replied. "Fancies himself a gunman."

"That he does," Resnick said, starting to wonder if O'Shay wasn't the least of his problems.

"Then he was here?"

"Was . . . and is."

"Where?"

The lawman stared at the Gunsmith and said, "You know, I haven't the faintest idea."

"He's not registered at the hotel?"

"No."

"Is there a boardinghouse in town?"

"He's not there either."

"Where else could he be, then?"

Resnick had an idea, but he didn't present it for the Gunsmith's benefit.

"He could be working at one of the ranches."

"Has he killed anyone while he's been here?"

The sheriff nodded.

"Yesterday. He killed a man yesterday."

"Fair fight?"

"That's what witnesses called it."

Five, Clint thought, that makes five.

"What did you do?"

"What could I do?" Resnick asked, raising his hands helplessly. "I never was and never will be the lawman you were, Adams. I didn't want this job, anyway."

"But you've got it."

"Yeah," the lawman said, "I've got it. I talked to him, he listened, and then he did what he wanted to."

"Which was?"

Resnick shrugged. "He said he was staying, but he didn't say where. Sorry I can't help you more."

"You've helped me plenty."

Clint turned and started for the door, but the sheriff pulled him up short.

"Adams."

"Yes?"

"What do you intend to do with this O'Shay? Kill him?"

"I hope not," Clint said. "I'm hoping to keep him from killing anyone else."

Resnick shrugged helplessly and asked, "You wouldn't be looking for a red-haired woman, would you?"

Clint frowned at the question and said, "No, but I wouldn't throw one back if I found one."

As the Gunsmith left the office, the lawman's eyes took on a dreamy look and he said, "Especially not this one."

Satisfied that Danny O'Shay was somewhere around Pleasant Point, Clint put Duke up at the livery and then went to register at the hotel.

Signing in, he checked the register book himself for
Danny O'Shay's name, but the only thing of interest he
found was a single name signed in a bold hand: *Scarlet*.
Clint had the distinct feeling that the name should have
been signed in red—bright, blood red.

"Who's this?" he asked, turning the register around
and pointing out the name to the clerk.

"That's a lady who registered a couple of days
ago," the man replied, a faraway look coming into his
eyes, "and what a lady she is."

"Is she a redhead?" Clint asked on a hunch.

"Do you know her?"

"No."

"You'll want to," the clerk assured him.

"That remains to be seen," Clint said, taking his
key from the man. "Thanks."

ELEVEN

Patience is a virtue that few people possess in abundance.

It had been two days since the Titus hands had approached her in the hotel dining room, and she was beginning to believe that they *hadn't* been sent by their boss. In fact, she had heard some talk around town that the men had been fired for their actions.

That didn't fit her picture of John Titus—unless he had something up his sleeve.

She was growing impatient to find out.

Danny O'Shay's patience—never one of the young man's virtues—was wearing very thin. It had been three days since he'd killed the man from the Barrow ranch. He still didn't know why, but that wasn't important to him. The only thing he felt was important was when he'd get to use his gun again.

If Titus didn't give him the word soon, he was going to do it on his own.

John Titus was growing impatient waiting for the man

he'd sent for by telegram, a man whose services he had used before and now needed again.

He was aware that O'Shay was getting edgy, which was dangerous. He could let the young would-be gunman go after Barrow himself, but Titus was concerned about the woman. What was she waiting for? When would she make her move? If it wasn't soon, then he was going to have to move against her first, and then Barrow, and hope that nothing went wrong.

He hoped that the man he sent for would arrive within a day or two because beyond that, things might just get out of control.

John Titus couldn't afford that. He had to be in control every step of the way and, with luck, he would be again—soon.

Sheriff Bill Resnick wondered how John Titus would react if he were to ask to be allowed to resign. Having Danny O'Shay, the red-haired woman who called herself Scarlet, and the Gunsmith in town at the same time was more than Bill Resnick could even think about handling.

First things first, however. He had to send a message to Titus that the Gunsmith was in town. He wondered how old John Titus would react to that little piece of news.

Frank Valin didn't relish relaying this piece of news to Titus. In fact, he was getting tired of playing messenger. He was supposed to be foreman of Titus's Big-T spread, but he was being reduced to running messages back and forth from town.

Things had to change soon, but for now there was *another* message to be presented to Titus.

"What have you got to tell me now, Valin?" Titus demanded wearily.

The foreman noticed that the strain was beginning to tell on the older man—who was looking older. "There's another stranger in town."

"The woman is still there?"

"She hasn't left," Valin said, "but I think you'll find this arrival a little interesting."

"All right, all right," Titus said, "since you're obviously busting to tell me who it is, go ahead and tell me!"

"His name's Clint Adams," Frank Valin said, "but they call him—"

"—the Gunsmith!" Titus said, finishing for the other man. "What does he want?"

"He was asking the sheriff about Danny O'Shay."

"O'Shay?" Titus repeated. "That kid?"

"That's what Resnick said," Valin answered, "and by the way, our sheriff is getting pretty nervous with all these strangers in town."

"I'm not worried about Resnick," Titus said absently. "I'm more interested in the Gunsmith asking for O'Shay. Do you know what that means?"

"What?"

"That we may have misjudged this kid," Titus said, rubbing his jaw.

"What do you mean?"

"He said he learned how to use a gun from the Gunsmith," Titus reminded his foreman, "and now the Gunsmith arrives in town looking for him. What does that tell you?"

Valin shrugged.

Impatiently, Titus said, "It's obvious that they know each other. O'Shay might be better with a gun than we thought.''

"But you sent for—''

"I know who I sent for, Frank, but now I know what I've got, as well. This could work out for the best.''

"How?''

"Maybe I can parlay this into a winning hand,'' Titus said. "O'Shay takes care of Barrow while the Gunsmith takes care of the woman.''

"What makes you think he'd do that?''

"The man has a big reputation, Frank,'' Titus said. "All I have to do is offer him enough money,'' Titus went on confidently, "and he'll take care of her. He didn't get that rep by turning down offers like this. Even a living legend needs money.''

"Boss—''

"This could work out, Valin,'' Titus said, ignoring Valin's attempt to speak, "this could actually work out to our advantage.''

"Mr. Titus—''

"I want you to go to town and invite the Gunsmith here,'' Valin went on. "Tell him we'll make it well worth his while. Make damn sure he knows there's money in it.''

"When do you want him?''

"The sooner the better.''

"Yes, sir.''

"All right, get moving.''

"Boss, can we talk—''

"Later, Valin,'' Titus snapped. "I've got to think this through. Leave me alone.''

Valin wanted to argue but the other man was already in a world of his own.

After the foreman left, John Titus sat back in his chair,

rubbing his hands together. The Gunsmith riding into Pleasant Point was a godsend, and he was determined to make the most of it.

TWELVE

Clint decided to have lunch before he started his search for Danny O'Shay, and the hotel dining room seemed as good a place as any.

He noticed the redhead as soon as he walked in. She seemed to be getting extra special service from a nervous waiter, and more than one man in the room was watching her, for obvious reasons.

Her hair was like fire and her green eyes like ice, staring down any man who met her gaze. Even though she was seated, he could see that she was tall, full of breast and hip, and long-legged. She was one of the finest-looking women he had seen in a long time.

Briefly, he entertained the idea of approaching her, but that wasn't what he was there for. Another time, maybe—no, definitely—but not now.

He gave his order to a second waiter and as he started on his lunch three men who didn't look as if they were there to eat entered the room.

He watched as their eyes raked the room, stopped briefly at the redhead, then moved on until they came to rest on him. The man in the center, the largest of the

three and obviously the man in charge, said something
to the other two then started toward Clint's table while
the others occupied a empty table by the door.

"Mr. Adams?"

"That's right."

"May I sit down?"

Right off Clint felt the man's polite manner was not
natural, which meant he would have preferred to be
somewhere else, probably playing cards or having a
drink.

"If you can give me a good reason why I should say
yes," Clint replied.

A muscle jumped in the man's cheek and he said,
"Well, I suppose the best reason for anything might be
money."

"How much money?"

"A lot."

"Should we start by having you pay for my lunch?"

That muscle jumped again—twice this time—before
the man said, "Why not?"

"Why don't you have a seat?"

The man sat down, and Clint continued to eat his
lunch.

"Would you like to start with your name?"

"My name is Frank Valin. I'm the foreman of the
Big-T spread."

"Who owns that?"

"John Titus."

"Never heard of him," the Gunsmith lied.

Clint found it funny that his remark didn't cause the
muscle in the man's cheek to jump. Could it be that he
didn't like his boss?

"He's a big man in these parts."

"Well, good for him. I suppose, then, that you're here on his behalf."

"What?"

"He sent you."

"Oh, yeah, he did."

"What's it about?"

"Mr. Titus would like you to come out to the ranch as soon as possible."

"For dinner?"

Valin frowned and said, "I suppose—"

"No, I mean did he send you here just to invite me to dinner?"

"Oh, no. He wants to talk to you."

"About what?"

"A job."

"I don't need a job."

"Well, when you hear Mr. Titus's offer, you might decide that you want this one."

"Can you tell me anything else about it?"

"Only that it could mean a lot of money to you."

"I see."

"And it might lead you to Danny O'Shay."

"Is that a fact?"

If Valin knew he was looking for O'Shay, that meant that the sheriff was on John Titus's payroll, because the lawman was the only person he'd mentioned Danny O'Shay to.

"Well, then, maybe I should go out and see what your boss has to offer."

"Good," Valin said, standing up.

"But not right now."

"When, then?" Valin asked, frowning.

"This evening," Clint said, "for dinner."

Valin seemed about to argue but he simply shrugged and said, "All right, I'll tell him. Ask anybody how to get out to the ranch."

"I will."

Valin nodded, didn't seem to know what to say next, then simply turned and walked away.

"Oh, and Valin."

"Yeah?"

"Tell him I like chicken."

Scarlet didn't know who the man having lunch was, but the other man had been pointed out to her by a helpful townsman as the foreman of the Big-T spread—John Titus's ranch.

The man having lunch looked like a type she had seen before. He'd be good with a gun, generally capable—and for hire.

His byplay with the Big-T foreman had seemed amiable enough, although the foreman had looked confused toward the end. Had Titus made his move? Was this man someone the rancher had hired for his gun?

She looked over at the man, who caught her eyes and looked back. She held his gaze for a moment, and when he smiled, she looked down at her empty plate.

He was attractive. She had not noticed that about a man in quite some time, but it didn't matter. If he was a gun for hire working for Titus, she was going to have to kill him, attractive or not.

She decided that she would try and find out who he was, and the best way to do that was to check at the hotel desk. He would have signed in after her, and once she had his name, she could decide what her next move should be.

She called the waiter over, paid him, then left the dining room without looking at the other man again. She went directly to the front desk and asked the flustered clerk for the register.

There was only one name that had been entered after hers: Clint Adams.

The Gunsmith!

What was he doing in Pleasant Point? Could he really be working for someone like John Titus?

Her heart began to beat faster—uncontrollably so—as she realized that to get to John Titus, she was first going to have to kill the legendary Gunsmith.

Or die trying.

Valin returned immediately to the ranch to tell Titus the Gunsmith had accepted his invitation. "I think he's gonna want to see O'Shay," the foreman finished.

"O'Shay? You didn't mention him, did you?"

"Uh, no, sir," Valin lied.

"Good. Maybe if Adams thinks he's going to O'Shay, he'll take the job and stay around longer. Did he say what time he'd be here?"

"Uh, for dinner."

"Dinner?" Titus asked, frowning. "Did I say to invite him to dinner?"

"It just seemed . . . to be a good idea," Valin blustered.

"Actually, it is a good idea, Frank," Titus said, looking at his foreman with surprise. The man was a good foreman and knew how to run the ranch, but beyond that he had never demonstrated an ability to think on his feet. "I'll tell the cook."

"Chicken," Valin said.

"What?"

"Uh, I think it would be better if the cook made chicken."

"Why?"

"Adams was, uh, having chicken for lunch."

"Why would he want it for dinner?"

"I heard him say that he loves chicken."

"Chicken it is, then," Titus said. "If he takes my offer, he can have all the chicken he wants." Titus started to leave the room, then turned and said to Valin, "Thanks, Frank."

"Sure, Boss."

Frank Valin couldn't believe that after all these years he had made his biggest impression on Titus with an idea that was the Gunsmith's, not his.

Hiring a man for a killing, over dinner.

Clint wouldn't have accepted John Titus's invitation if it wasn't for the fact that Valin had mentioned Danny O'Shay. Of course, that didn't mean that seeing Titus would actually be a means to locating O'Shay, but Clint was willing to take the chance.

It wasn't hard to guess what Titus wanted to hire him to do. After all, a big rancher does have a need every now and then for a gun hand. Clint decided he would listen very politely to his offer and then try to find out where O'Shay was *before* turning the man down.

His other interest in town had become the red-haired woman. She had been looking at him strangely in the dining room just before she got up and left. Also, it seemed to him that Valin had exhibited more than a passing interest in her when he'd first entered the room.

Perhaps it would be wise, he thought, if he did take the time to make her acquaintance, after all.

Scarlet was thinking along the same lines.

She had no illusions about her abilities with a gun. She had drilled and drilled, teaching herself everything she thought she needed to know, until she felt secure enough to start her search for the five men who had wiped out her family. She was sure she could handle herself against most men with a gun.

The Gunsmith, however, was not most men.

Believing she had a chance in hell of outdrawing the Gunsmith would have been an illusion, and Scarlet had been dealing in reality ever since the first of those five men raped her.

She figured her best bet was to present herself to the Gunsmith, find out if he was indeed working for John Titus, then try and sway him to her side—using whatever means necessary.

As a young girl, sex had been something mysterious to her, something she'd been told by her mother would be a wonderful thing to be shared with the man she loved. Those five men stole that from her when she was seventeen, and now sex was simply something else she used to get to where she was going. It was a tool, like her horse, and her gun.

And it was perhaps the tool she knew how to use best.

THIRTEEN

Frank Valin had been right. Apparently everybody knew where the Titus ranch was. The first person Clint asked—the desk clerk—gave him directions. It seemed that about ten minutes after he left town, he'd be on Titus land.

That was impressive. What was also impressive was the fact that it had only taken Titus four years to amass that much land.

He decided to do some research before going out to Titus's house for dinner. He checked out all of the property Titus had acquired and discovered it had been bought and paid for, all legal.

He thought it odd that John Titus might want to hire a gun after four years of playing it legal. Clint had known a lot of big ranchers who used professional guns to acquire anything they wanted. The difference with Titus had to be his political ambitions. Because of that, he was trying to stay on the clean side of the law.

Why change now? he wondered. Why hire Danny O'Shay as a gunman, then go after someone like the

Gunsmith? What was happening in John Titus's life now that would make him go this route?

Or was his assumption as to why Titus wanted to see him wrong?

There was only one way to find out.

When Clint went up to his room to change clothes, he found the door ajar. There was someone waiting inside, but he knew if they were waiting to do him harm, they would have made sure the door was closed.

He stepped in with his gun still holstered. Seated on his bed was the red-haired woman identified in the register as Scarlet.

"Miss Scarlet, I presume."

"That's right."

Clint had found women in his room countless times before, many of them there for nothing but pleasure and most of those already undraped. Scarlet was fully dressed, right down to the cartridge belt around her waist.

"You know who I am," she said.

"Well, that would seem to make us even, wouldn't it?" Clint asked.

She didn't answer. Up close like this, in a smaller room, her beauty was stunning. The effect of her green eyes, however, was still that of two blocks of ice.

"Is there something I can help you with?"

"I saw you talking to John Titus's foreman in the dining room."

"That's right."

"Are you going to work for Titus?"

Clint, still standing, asked, "Why is that any of your business?"

Her cold eyes bored into his for a few moments, but

he stood his ground. He had the impression that this was a new experience for her.

"All I can tell you is that I have a stake in your decision."

"What decision?"

"To work for John Titus."

"I haven't even been offered a job yet," he said, "let alone accepted one."

"You haven't?" she asked, and for the first time since he'd laid eyes on her, her expression changed. She seemed confused.

"No, I haven't."

"Then what—"

"I'm going out to his ranch to talk to him," Clint explained, "but whether or not he offers me a job remains to be seen."

She got up from the bed abruptly and headed straight past him for the door.

"Hey, hold on a second, lady," he said, turning to watch her.

At the door she turned and faced him, looking very determined.

"Keep me in mind, please, when he offers to hire you for your gun."

"I don't hire my gun out, Miss—look, is Scarlet your first name or last name?"

"It's my name," she said. "Mr. Adams, I can offer you a lot of good reasons not to take a job working for John Titus, but the best one is simply this: I intend to kill him."

"I see."

"I know who you are," she went on, "but I have to tell you that if you get between him and me, I'll have to try and kill you too."

She had a lot of sand, this lady. She knew who he was and she was threatening him.

"Do you think you could, Scarlet?"

"Frankly," she said, "no, but that doesn't mean I won't try. I've got too much at stake here to back away from a gunfight, even if it's with you."

He regarded her for a moment and then said, "Look, why don't we talk again after I come back from talking to Titus. Will you have breakfast with me in the morning?"

"Why wait that long?" she asked. "I'm room thirteen. Come and see me when you get back. Maybe I can give you another reason, as well."

After she left he realized that she'd been offering to go to bed with him, but he could recall having been threatened in warmer tones than she'd used to offer him sex.

FOURTEEN

John Titus's house was as impressive as the size of his spread. It was a two-story structure with a porch as wide as the house itself.

There was a ranch hand waiting in front of the building as the light began to fade, and he was suitably impressed when Clint handed him Duke's reins.

"I assume I'll be here for awhile," Clint said. "Unsaddle him and give him some feed. Don't do anything else, and above all don't try to ride him."

"I wouldn't—"

"Just do what I've told you and he won't hurt you."

"Hurt me?"

"He's got a mind of his own," Clint said, giving the big black an affectionate pat. "I'll see you later, big fella."

The huge gelding bobbed his head up and down, causing the hand to back away.

"Be nice," Clint said, and stepped up onto the huge front porch.

As he approached the front door, it opened and a man stepped out. The man was tall, slender, and white-haired, although he appeared to Clint to be not much older than himself. "Mr. Adams?" he said.

"That's right."

The man extended his hand and said, "I'm John Titus. Welcome to my house."

"Thank you," Clint said, accepting the proffered hand. "You have a beautiful place."

Looking pleased, Titus said, "I built it myself. Come inside, dinner is ready."

Titus led Clint to a huge dining room with a long table covered with a white tablecloth. As they seated themselves a houseman came out, served them soup and poured them wine.

"Are we eating alone?"

"I live alone," Titus said.

"I thought perhaps your foreman—"

"He eats with the hands."

"Is Danny O'Shay one of your hands?"

"No," Titus said without looking up from his soup.

"I was given to understand that he was."

"Would you like to discuss business during dinner, or after?"

"Do we have business to discuss?"

"I have an offer to make."

"Then make it."

Titus wiped his mouth with a white cloth napkin and looked at the Gunsmith.

"I want to hire you."

"To do what?"

"I would think that was obvious."

"It isn't to me."

"Your reputation—"

"Means very little to me," Clint said, interrupting.

"The only people impressed with reputations, Mr. Titus, are those who don't have any."

"I don't understand," Titus said, looking puzzled.

"You are Clint Adams, the Gunsmith, aren't you?"

"I am."

Looking visibly relieved, Titus said, "Good. I thought I might have had the wrong man."

"You still may," Clint said.

The two men stared at each other from opposite ends of the ten-foot table as the houseman entered the room again. He looked at Titus, who nodded, and the man proceeded to clear the soup dishes.

"Maybe you'd better make your offer, Mr. Titus, before he brings the main course."

Titus drummed his fingers on the table, obviously wondering if he should waste a meal on a man who might turn down his offer afterward.

"Very well," he said, making his decision. "I want to hire your gun."

"That's fine," Clint said, putting his cloth napkin down on the table and standing up.

"I don't understand."

"I don't hire my gun out, Titus."

"But—"

"I want to see Danny O'Shay."

Titus's face took on a stern cast and he said, "I don't know anyone by that name."

"Your foreman said different."

Annoyance flickered across his face briefly before Titus replied, "Then he was wrong."

"I don't think so."

Titus stood up and said, "I'll have to ask you to leave my house."

"What do you know about a woman named Scarlet?"

"I don't know any such woman."

"A red-haired woman in her early twenties, green eyes—" Clint said, beginning to describe Scarlet, but Titus gave him no chance to finish.

"Don't make me force you to leave."

Clint knew that Titus had a lot of men working for him. For all he knew, some of them were hidden now, with guns trained on him.

"I'm leaving, Titus," Clint said, "but I'll be back."

"Come back anytime," Titus said, and then added, "anytime you're ready to work for me. I'll pay good money, Adams. Probably more than you've ever seen in one place at one time."

"You don't have enough money to buy my gun, Titus," Clint said. "Believe me."

Angry that a man with a reputation as a common gunman would get so high and mighty with him, Titus answered smugly, "I've got enough money to buy any gun I want, Adams."

"Not mine."

"Then I'll buy one better."

"You're welcome to try."

"Get out."

Clint left the house, found Duke in the barn, saddled him up and rode out, all the while waiting for someone to make a move on him.

No one did.

After the Gunsmith left, the houseman came into the dining room bearing a tray with two plates of chicken.

As he approached the table to set them down, Titus swung his arm viciously, knocking the tray from the elderly black man's hands and sending both plates of food crashing to the floor.

"Mr. Titus—"

"Shut up and go get me Valin—now!"

The man scurried from the room.

Titus sat and stewed until Valin arrived, obviously surprised not to find Clint Adams there.

"What happened?" he asked.

"I made a mistake," Titus said.

"What?"

"I let him go." Titus looked at Valin and said, "If he's not working for me, he's going to be working against me. I should have had men here ready to take care of him when he refused."

"He refused?"

"Yes he refused!" Titus shouted, his face suffused with blood.

"Maybe he'll just move on—"

"And maybe he won't!" Titus shot back. "I can't take that chance. Frank, he just left. Take a couple of men and go after him."

"Wha—"

Titus glared at his foreman hotly and said, "I don't want him to reach town alive, Valin. Understand?"

"Yes, sir."

And as an afterthought he flung after the man, "And don't do it on my land!"

They didn't do it on anyone's land.

Clint Adams, uneasy because he'd been able to walk away from the Titus ranch so easily, pushed Duke as hard as he dared push him while traveling in unfamiliar territory—in the dark—and Frank Valin and his two men, riding three of the Big-T's finest horses, were never able to catch up.

FIFTEEN

When Clint knocked on the door of room 13, it was opened immediately by Scarlet, dressed exactly as she had been when he saw her earlier.

"You waited up for me," he said, stepping past her into the room.

"You're early," she said, closing the door behind them. She was ill at ease at being alone in her room with him.

"What happened?" she asked, eyeing him coldly—although he thought he could detect some anxiety behind the ice. Still, he thought, it could have been his imagination.

"He offered me a job."

"Doing what?"

"He wanted my gun."

"Why?"

"I didn't ask."

"Did you take the job?"

"Do you think he's looking to hire a gun to take care of you, Scarlet?"

"I think that's exactly what he wants."

"Well," he said, "it won't be me."

"You turned down his offer?"

"I told you earlier," Clint said. "I don't hire out my gun."

Scarlet thought a moment, then said, "All right."

"That's it?"

"What else did you expect?"

He wanted to see some heat come to this woman's eyes, even if it was the heat of anger. "Well, you did make some promises," he said.

"Did I?"

"You inferred that there would be something else waiting for me here tonight."

She stared at him with absolutely no expression on her face and not a trace of heat in her eyes.

"You didn't strike me as the kind of man—" she began, but then stopped short, shrugged, and began to unbutton her shirt.

He watched, somewhat awed, as she undressed. First she removed everything above the belt, so that her firm, rounded breasts came into view with their large, russet-colored nipples. As he watched he became aware that it was cold in the room because her nipples were hardening, which he knew had nothing at all to do with him.

Next she removed her boots, then her pants, and in moments she was totally nude and had gooseflesh from the cold.

"There," she said, staring at him boldly.

Clint Adams had known many, many women over the years and had gotten to the point where he could actually smell a woman when she was ready. There was no such scent from Scarlet. She was naked and alone in a room with a man—modestly, not an unattractive man—and she was showing no interest whatsoever.

The challenge was unmistakable, and he knew that many men would have taken hold of her, thrown her down on the bed, and thoroughly fucked her, whether *she* enjoyed it or not. But he was not many men. For Clint Adams part of sex was knowing that his partner was enjoying it as much as he was.

There would be no such shared enjoyment here.

Although his penis was fully erect and pushing painfully against his pants, he said, "Not tonight, thanks," turned and walked out.

Out in the hallway, between his room and the room he'd just left, Clint Adams stopped short, shook his head admiringly and said, "Damn, Adams, you've got willpower!"

He entered his room, impressed with himself—and angry with himself—and became even more angry when a bullet gouged out a piece of the door near his head. He launched himself into a dive that took him to the right of the bed and came up with gun in hand, pointed across the mattress at the window, where the shot had come from.

He stayed that way for a few moments, until he heard footsteps in the hallway approaching his room. It was obvious that the single shot was all that was coming and, having failed, whoever had fired it was long gone.

"What happened?" Scarlet asked as she rushed into the room. The only light at that moment was coming from the lamps in the hallway, now blocked by the redhead, who was fully dressed.

"Let's get some light," he said, standing up and walking to the lamp near the door.

He turned up the flame as people from other rooms poked their heads outside.

"It's all over, folks," Clint said. He took Scarlet's elbow and pulled her into the room. "Thanks very much for your concern," he told the others and shut the door in their faces.

"Are you all right?" she asked.

"I'm touched by your concern," he remarked, observing that there was no sign of that concern in her eyes or on her lovely face.

He holstered his gun and walked to the window. Although he had left it closed, it was now open, obviously having been forced. He peered outside, saw nothing, then drew his head and shoulders back in and closed the window.

"I'm fine," he said, walking to the door to inspect the bullet hole. The slug had gouged out a piece of the door right at the edge, then ricocheted off somewhere. He'd look for it in the morning.

"I guess this is what you get for turning down John Titus's offer," Scarlet observed.

"You think Titus was behind this?"

"You don't?"

"I've got a lot of enemies in the world, ma'am," he told her, "and there are a lot of other people who don't know me but would get a real kick out of becoming known as the person who killed me."

She shook her head and said, "Titus. If you're not working for him, you're working against him. That's the way he'd see it. With me around he's got to figure he doesn't need the added threat of you."

"And why are you a threat to him?"

"I told you. I intend to kill him."

"No," Clint said, "I mean why?"

"Well," she said, moving toward the door, "if you're all right I'll get back to my room. It's getting late."

"You don't like to have bags under your eyes when you kill someone?"

"Oh, I won't kill him tomorrow," she said. "He'll have to wait for it."

"And what about the answer to my question?"

"I guess," she said, opening the door, "you'll just have to wait too."

"Until you know me better?"

She looked at him, said, "Just until," and left.

Clint Adams took certain precautions to make sure that he would be able to get a good night's sleep—perching a basin on the windowsill and setting a chair against the door—then crawled between the sheets, which had grown cold because the window had been open so long.

He knew of a way to warm them up quickly, but he supposed that would also have to wait "until."

SIXTEEN

It wasn't until morning that Frank Valin reported to Titus.

"What happened?" Titus demanded when Valin returned to the house.

"Uh—"

"Where were you all night?" Titus continued. "Is he dead?"

Valin hesitated as long as he possibly could, but knew he had to answer, so he finally said, "No."

"What!"

"He's not dead."

"Why not?" Titus demanded, slamming his fists down on his desk.

"We couldn't catch him, Mr. Titus," Valin complained. "You saw that horse he rides. He must have let him out full going to town."

"He knew," Titus said, waving a finger in the air. "He knew, dammit, that I'd send somebody after him. God dammit, that makes him even more dangerous than before. He's got to be killed, Valin."

"What about your man—"

"If he arrives today, fine," Titus said, "but tell me what else happened. Why were you so late coming back?"

"We made a try for him at his hotel."

"And what happened?"

"We missed."

"Did anyone see you?" Titus asked anxiously.

"No."

"You're sure?"

"Yes."

Little by little John Titus saw his political ambitions melting away, first because of that damn girl, and now because of the Gunsmith. . . .

"Valin, you and I know who I've sent for," Titus said, "*only* you and I. He should arrive here today. Go to town and wait for him."

"To town?" Valin asked nervously. "After what happened—"

"Take some men."

"Mr. Titus—"

"All right," Titus said angrily. "Where do you have O'Shay?"

"He's at the line shack up on—"

"Go and get me O'Shay," Titus said, interrupting him. "Let's find out just what kind of relationship he had with the Gunsmith."

"It's about time you sent for me, Mr. Titus," Danny O'Shay said boldly. "It's been days since I shot down that cowpoke—"

"You did real good, Danny," Titus said, looking past him at Valin, who was standing behind the young

man. He nodded, indicating that he wanted the foreman to stay.

"Are you ready to use me again?" the boy asked,
his eagerness showing in his voice and in his eyes.

"That depends."

"On what?"

"On what you can tell me about the Gunsmith."

"What do you want to know?"

"How well do you know him?"

O'Shay shrugged and said, "Real well."

"Are you friends?"

Danny frowned and asked, "What's this all about,
Mr. Titus? Why all the questions about the
Gunsmith?"

"He's in town, Danny," Titus said, studying the
boy's face for a reaction, "and he's in my way."

"He's in Pleasant Point?"

"Yes. Does that bother you?"

"No," O'Shay said, shrugging again, "it don't
bother me. Why should it?"

"Danny, let's stop playing games," Titus said.
"You told Valin and me that you learned how to use a
gun from the Gunsmith."

"That's right."

"Doesn't that make you friends?"

"No, it don't."

"Then if I wanted you to take the Gunsmith out of
my way, you'd be able to do it?"

O'Shay didn't answer right away, then with an un-
successful attempt at bravado said, "Sure."

Titus doubted that O'Shay could take the
Gunsmith—alone, anyway.

"All right, O'Shay," he said, "I want you to go to

town with Mr. Valin and do exactly what he tells you. If he tells you to kill another Barrow hand, you'll do it, won't you?''

"Sure."

"And if he tells you to throw down on the Gunsmith would you do that?''

"Alo—'' O'Shay began, and Titus knew he was about to ask ''Alone?'' and thought better of it. Instead he said, ''Yeah, I would.''

"All right, Danny. Go out to the bunkhouse. Valin will come and get you.''

"Sure, Mr. Titus.''

When Danny O'Shay left Titus's office, he wasn't so sure he'd done the right thing, but between the house and the bunkhouse he convinced himself that he had.

He knew now why the Gunsmith had refused to work with him with a gun in Hedgemont: Clint Adams was afraid of him. He was afraid that Danny might actually be better than him.

Maybe the Gunsmith had the big rep now, Danny O'Shay thought, but all he had to do was kill him and then *he'd* have the big rep.

He'd show Clint Adams that he didn't need any help with a gun. He knew how to use one just fine.

"What do you think?" Titus asked Valin.

"I think he's full of horseshit, Boss.''

"You take him to town with you, anyway,'' Titus ordered the foreman. ''He's killed men already, so that means he knows how. Take a few other men too. If it comes to it, all of you will have to take care of the Gunsmith, and O'Shay's gun might come in handy.''

Valin decided to take O'Shay and three others. Surely five men were enough to draw down on one man, even if he was a legend.

Weren't they?

Ross Bowman was an hour outside of Pleasant Point, Nevada. In his shirt pocket was the telegram from his old friend, John Titus—only he wasn't Ross Bowman when he knew Titus, and for that matter, Titus wasn't John Titus. Still, the names they had then weren't so far from the names they went by now.

Bowman and Titus had done the best of the five they were back then. Two of the five were dead— killed, it was said, by a woman. The fifth man had faded from sight, and maybe he was dead too.

John Titus was a powerful rancher who, from time to time, needed the services of ''Ross Bowman,'' who had become very successful at making his way with a gun.

Bowman hadn't liked the tone of Titus's telegram. It was a little too . . . desperate. Whatever was wrong this time, the would-be politician knew no other way to handle it than to call for Bowman.

He patted the pocket with the telegram, then spurred his horse forward, to cover the final hour that lay between him and the problem that existed for ''John Titus'' in Pleasant Point.

Scarlet did something that night that she hadn't done in years.

She dreamt about a man.

She dreamt about Clint Adams.

In her dream she was standing there naked before

him, as she had in her room that night, only this time he didn't just turn around and leave. This time he moved toward her, put his hands on her breasts, pushed her back to the bed, and fell on top of her.

In her dream he was suddenly as naked as she was . . .

. . . and she woke up sweating, heart pounding, angry with herself for having such a dream . . . and angry for another reason.

She realized, sitting there in bed with her nipples erect, that she hadn't wanted him to leave last night, and she couldn't understand that.

What made this man so different from all of the others? She'd gone to bed with men before, for different reasons, and she'd been able to perform without feeling anything. Last night she'd *wanted* to feel something.

For the first time since she was seventeen, she wanted to feel something other than the hunger for revenge.

Was it Clint Adams . . . or was it just time?

Maybe she should find out.

Clint awoke that morning instantly alert. His eyes moved first to the basin on the window and then to the chair against the door. Both were intact.

He swung his feet to the floor and made use of the slop bucket beneath the bed. Unbidden, the image of Scarlet making use of such a bucket sprang to mind, and he dispelled it with a shake of his head. He removed the basin from the windowsill and put it to the use it was meant for. When he was fully awake and dressed, he went down the hall to invite the lady to breakfast.

Remembering how she had come rushing into his room last night after the shot—she had dressed pretty quick to do it—he had a feeling she would accept.

SEVENTEEN

"Why did you accept my invitation to breakfast?" he asked her later, unable to contain the question any longer.

She hesitated a moment and then said, "I don't rightly know."

There was something new in her eyes. He actually thought he detected some sign of a thaw.

"I dreamt about you last night," she said, breaking the silence.

"Really?" he asked. "I'm flattered. That sounds like an admission for a woman like you to make."

Her eyes flashed this time and she demanded, "What do you know about the kind of woman I am?"

"Do you want me to tell you?"

"Yes!"

"You're very beautiful," he said, "but then you know that. I think you're also very determined, and I think that you've been hurt sometime in your past and now you're out to settle an old score."

When she didn't respond, he knew he'd filled in his hand and asked, "How'd I do?"

"You did well," she said. "You did real good. I guess you're real smart, aren't you?"

"I never considered my brains one of my strong points," he said. "If it was . . ."

"If it was . . . what?"

"Never mind."

"No, no," she argued, "you started to say something, now finish it."

"If I was a smart man," he said, "I never would have gotten saddled with being called . . . the Gunsmith."

"That happened a long time ago, didn't it?" she asked. "When you were young?"

"Very young," he said, "and still fairly new to the west. I knew about guns, though, and everything else just sort of came along."

"You weren't born here in the west?"

"No," he said, "in the east . . . somewhere. Don't rightly recall where."

"Or maybe you just don't want to say."

"Maybe."

"What's it like having the reputation like you do?" she asked, looking very interested in the answer.

"Hell," he said. "It's like a living hell on earth. Let me give you some advice, Scarlet. If you've got a score to settle, then settle it, but don't make a big thing out of it publicly. Don't get yourself a reputation—although I guess it will be hard for you not to."

"Why do you say that?"

"Like I said before, you're beautiful, you've got that flaming red hair, and a woman with a gun—if she knows how to use it—is just naturally going to be noticed." He stopped a moment and then said, "You've killed already, haven't you?"

She didn't answer right away, then nodded and said, "Yes, twice."

"For good reason?"

"For a real good reason."

"And is that why you're here for Titus? To kill him for a similar reason?"

"The same exact reason."

"And how many more after him?"

"Two."

"And then what?"

The question startled her.

"I—I don't know. I've never thought about what would happen . . . after."

"Well, think about it, and think about it hard. Take my word for it, after you've killed that many men—I assume they're all men?"

"They are."

"After you've killed that many men, it's not going to be easy to go back to . . . to whatever life you had before."

"I didn't have a life before this," she said. "None to go back to, anyway."

"A home?"

"No."

"Family?"

She winced and said, "No."

"I'm sorry," he said, realizing that the conversation was becoming painful for her. "I really don't mean to pry, but I like you."

She looked at him as if he was crazy and said, "How can you like me? You don't even know me."

"That's true enough," he said, "and you don't know me, either, but here we are having breakfast, just like two old friends."

She stared at him, her green eyes holding steady and then suddenly wavering and misting over. It was only a hint of mist, though, and suddenly it was gone and her eyes were cold again.

"Tell me something, Adams," she said, "just how curious are you?"

"About you?"

She nodded.

"Not curious enough to force you to talk if you don't want to, Scarlet," he answered, "but curious enough to listen if you *want* to talk."

"And why would I want to do that?"

"Because," he said, leaning his elbows on the table, "because maybe you haven't talked to anyone in a long time, and you need to."

"All right," she said, as if she'd already decided earlier, "all right, but you asked for it, so don't stop me before the story is finished."

"I won't stop you," he said. "You'll stop when you're ready."

"Not here, though," she said. "This is too public. Are you finished?"

"I'm finished."

"Then let's go to my room and make ourselves comfortable," she said, "and I'll tell you my tale of woe."

EIGHTEEN

At seventeen Scarlet knew she was very womanly, full of breast and hip, with the added attraction of her obvious innocence. Her beauty eventually led to the slaughter of her family: her mother, father, two brothers, and younger sister.

One day, five men rode into town (whose name and location Scarlet doesn't divulge to Clint) and spied her at the general store, helping her mother shop. A couple of the men made lewd remarks about her, to which her mother reacted by calling them names and angering them. Later, when her mother related the story to her father, he wanted to go to town with a shotgun, but they prevailed upon him not to.

Sometime later, the five men rode up to her father's ranch. Scarlet did not yet know that they had robbed the bank in town, killed a lawman, and had then headed straight for her ranch. Prior to the robbery, they had inquired in town about who in the area raised the finest horses, and were told that Scarlet's father had the finest stock. (Again, as with the name of the town, Scarlet was careful not to tell Clint her father's full name.)

The men shot down on her father before he had a chance to grab his shotgun. Her brothers—although younger than her—had bravely tried to resist, but they were struck down with ease.

When the men saw Scarlet, they recognized her from town. Not only did they take turns raping her, but her younger sister, as well, who at the time was only thirteen but a red-haired beauty in her own right; and her mother, who in her forties was still a handsome woman.

Afterward, they shot each of the women and left, taking horses, money, and whatever valuables they wanted from the house. . . .

"How can you possibly blame yourself for all of that, Scarlet?" Clint asked when she finished her story.

She stared at him, her face looking as if it had been chiseled from stone, and said, "I aroused their lust. If not for me, they would have taken what they wanted and left. While one was raping me, the others decided to use my mother and sister while waiting. I was the main target of their lust, however, and eventually they all used me. . . ."

"That must have been traumatic for you."

"I don't know what that means."

"A shock."

"Oh, it was a shock, all right, to lose my innocence that way, but it's been more of a shock for the men I've caught up with since then.

"They shot us and left us all for dead, but I didn't die. A neighbor came by and found me and took me to the doctor. I lived and I learned how to use a gun and whatever other tools I could so that I could take my vengeance and the vengeance of my family on them."

"You've found two so far, after all these years?"

"I never gave up," she said, "and when I found them I made sure they knew who I was before I killed them."

"And what of the others?" he asked. "Don't you think they heard about it and know that you're looking for them?"

"I'm sure they do."

"And Titus?" Clint asked. "He was one of the men?"

"Yes?"

"How did you find him?"

"The way I found the others," she said. "I kept looking, and kept listening, and investigated everything I heard. My father had a beautiful old flintlock, inlaid with silver. I understand that Titus—as he now calls himself—has it."

"You heard about it and came to have a look," he said. "What if it's not the same flintlock?"

"It was one of a kind."

"And what was Titus called then?"

"James Tillman," she said. "He used the same initials to begin his new life with the money he stole from the bank and whatever he stole from my family. I'll know him when I see him, though."

She had not shed a tear—nor misted over—during the entire story, but Clint suddenly had the impression that she was less tense.

"Are you all right?"

She sat on the bed, then looked up at him and said, "I'm fine. I think you were right. I needed to talk to someone about it." She hesitated a moment and then added, "Thank you." He knew those two words had not come easily to her.

"Scarlet, can I ask you something?"

"Why not?" she replied. "I've told you almost everything already."

"Have you . . . experienced any honest passion since then? Have you ever . . . enjoyed being with a man?"

She stared at him boldly and said, "I've had sex with men countless times since then, but to answer your question—no, I've never enjoyed it. I've never even *wanted* to enjoy it, until . . ."

"Until what?" he asked, moving closer to her but remaining standing. He didn't want to spook her now that she had taken him almost completely into her confidence.

She lowered her head, as if she could not meet his eyes, and said, "Until last night."

He put his hand on her shoulder, and she looked up at him.

"I didn't realize until later that I didn't want you to leave."

"Your body didn't react to the situation," he said, remembering how she'd been indifferent while naked and alone with him. "Your nipples hardened, but that was from the cold, and your . . . womanhood was dry, wasn't it?"

"Yes," she admitted, "but my body doesn't know how to react . . . Clint." She looked at him again and said, "I wanted you—God, I've never *wanted* a man before—but I didn't know how to show you, how to tell you . . ."

He sat next to her on the bed now, sliding his arm around her, and she dropped her head onto his shoulder.

"It's a simple thing, Scarlet, to let someone know

that you want them. You just have to react naturally.'' As if it were the most natural thing in the world he let his hand lay on her breasts.

"I don't react naturally anymore,'' she said, but he could feel her breath was quickening. Slowly, he undid the buttons of her shirt so he could slide his hand inside. She wasn't wearing any underclothes and his hand came into contact with the smooth flesh of her breast, then encountered her nipple, which responded to him this time, and not the cold.

She sighed, and he knew they were approaching a breakthrough.

"Scarlet.''

"Hmm?'' she mumbled dreamily.

He put his nose in her hair so that his mouth was next to her ear and he said, "I want to make love to you.'' The scent of her hair excited him. He kissed her ear, squeezing her breast, and then moved his lips to her neck.

"Oh,'' she said, and then as he slid his other hand into her shirt she said, "Yes.''

He finished unbuttoning her shirt and then removed it, dropping it on the floor. He kissed her neck and shoulder, fondling her breasts until her nipples were lust-swollen, and then he dipped his head so he could take first one and then the other into his mouth, sucking them, biting them, until she was moaning and clutching at his head.

"Clint . . .'' she gasped. "My God, I've never felt . . .''

"It's going to be good, honey,'' he said, unbuckling her gunbelt and her pants, "it's going to be very good. . . .''

He pushed her down so she was lying on the bed,

then removed her boots and slid off her pants. This time while she was naked he could smell her readiness. He eased his hand between her legs and found her moist. He found her clitoris, massaged it, and was surprised when she lifted her hips and climaxed with her eyes wide.

"What was that?" she asked when she caught breath.

"That was your body reacting honestly."

"I've never felt anything like that before."

"It gets better."

"Oh," she said in awe, "it couldn't. . . ."

He showed her that it could.

NINETEEN

He stood up and undressed, meaning to join her on the bed, but when his swollen penis came into view, standing straight up and prodding at the air, begging for release, she moaned and reached out to touch him. He stood by the bed while she first rubbed his rigid stalk, then squeezed it in her hands. She showed equal fascination with his balls, letting them lie in her palm like jewels of great value and even greater fragility.

"I've always thought of this part of a man as disgusting," she said, rubbing her thumb over the head of his cock while she held it tightly in one hand, "something that a man used to cause a woman pain."

"There is some pain involved at times," he said, "but only the best kind."

"I've used my mouth on men before," she went on, as if this were a rite of expiation, "but I've never enjoyed it, and I never wanted to."

"Do you want to now?"

"Yes," she said, her eyes glowing, and there it was! For the first time since he'd met her, there was heat in her eyes, an animal heat that caused them to glaze over slightly as her tongue flicked out to lick him like a hungry tabby.

"Mmmm, you taste marvelous, you smell marvelous. . . ." she murmered, licking the length of him. Finally, she opened her mouth and took him inside.

The sensation was exquisite as the spongy head of his penis slid past her lips and entered her mouth. She fondled his sac gently as she allowed even more of him to slide inside, and then her tongue was lashing him and her teeth were tattooing him. He looked down at her red hair, which seemed to be glowing, as if it were about to burst into flames. He reached down so that he could rub her breasts and nipples as she suckled him, and she moaned aloud and then sobbed as she sought to accommodate even more of him.

"Jesus, Scarlet," he said, feeling his toes beginning to curl, "I'm going to—"

"No," she said, allowing him to slide free finally. His penis glistened with her saliva, and the air cooled him. "I want you inside of me," she said, putting her hands on his buttocks and pulling him down to her. "Please . . ."

"There are other things I'd like to do," he said, "other things I'd like to show you. . . ."

"You can," she whispered, lifting her hips to him, "we have time, but first I want you inside of me. Oh, Clint, this is a new feeling for me, wanting a man . . ."

"Any man?"

"You!" she said, banging her pelvis against his demandingly.

"All right," he said. He kissed her and at the moment their lips met he entered her, sliding easily into her because of her moistness and his own saliva slickness.

She moaned into his mouth and he latched onto her tongue, sucking it as he drove himself into her, enjoying the feeling of her large breasts flattened between them, her hard nipples digging into his chest.

Her hands clasped the back of his head so that he couldn't break the kiss, and she began to chew on his tongue. The room was alive with the sound of their breath coming swiftly through their nostrils because neither one of them wanted to interrupt the kiss, even to breathe.

Her lips were the tastiest he'd ever encountered, and her tongue was equally delicious. He slid his hands beneath her to cup her buttocks and began to adjust his strokes, making them slower and longer, pausing as he reached the depths of her, and then withdrawing to pound into her again, and pause, and pound, and pause. . . .

Finally her lips slid away from his and she buried her face in his neck, sobbing and imploring him never to stop, biting his neck and his shoulders as her passion increased, climbing to a height she had never before reached.

And then she exploded beneath him as a massive climax took hold of her. She began to whip her head from side to side on the pillow while bouncing her buttocks out of his hand. He braced one hand on each side of her and continued to drive into her, looking down at her face and enjoying the look of pure animal pleasure he saw there. He felt a moment of great pride that *he* had been the one to put the heat in her eyes and that look on her face, to bring her pleasure she had never before experienced . . .

   . . . and then he was busy enjoying his own pleasure as his phallus swelled and exploded inside of her,
filling her with his milky seed and causing her to
climax a third time, even before the second one had
faded away. . . .

"Lord Jesus," she said, "what I've been missing all
these years. . . ."

"And more," he said. She was lying in the circle of
his arm and his hand was holding her breast, flicking at
the nipple with his thumb, enjoying the way the mound
of flesh seemed to fit there perfectly.

"All the more reason," she said, "for me to catch
the rest of those men and kill them. They made me miss
this—"

"Shh," he scolded her, "don't talk about that."

"Then make love to me again," she said, turning
toward him, "in a different way. Keep me from thinking, Clint. Love me."

He kissed her, holding her tightly against him, then
slid his lips down over her throat to her breasts. He
suckled her nipples for a long time, then continued his
journey down her magnificent body, knowing that he
was going to pleasure her again in a way she was totally
unfamiliar with.

Finally, his mouth was hovering near her fragrant
mound and he paused to breathe the heady scent of her
sex before plunging into her with his tongue.

"Oooh, God!" she moaned, lifting her butt off the
bed to meet the pressure of first his tongue and then his
lips as they sought her clit, latched onto it, and sucked
it. Slowly, tantalizingly, he encircled the stiff little nub

with his tongue while she clutched at the back of his head and pulled him tightly to her, as if seeking to drown him in her juices.

"Clint, ooh, yes, there . . . and there . . . yes, yes . . . oh, don't let it stop. . . ."

His tongue was lashing at her wildly now, his own passion increasing as he continued to savor the taste of her, and when he felt her belly begin to tremble, he sucked on her and literally yanked her climax from her.

She was bouncing up and down on the bed now, mindless in her joy of the moment. He got to his knees between her legs and pushed the head of his cock against her sex, and it was as if she sucked him in. She wrapped her long, powerful legs around his hips and he began to pound into her wildly, ruthlessly, just as mindlessly seeking his own gratification . . . and finding it.

Later they made love again, with her on top, and she seemed to enjoy the new position.

"I feel like I'm in charge," she said, sitting astride him and staring down at him. She had stopped riding him up and down, satisfied for the moment to simply feel him inside of her, pulsating, awaiting release.

He reached up and grasped her breasts, squeezing them, popping the nipples between his fingers.

"Harder," she said, closing her eyes and allowing her head to loll back, "squeeze them harder."

He obliged, squeezing them hard until, when he took his hands away, the marks of his fingers lingered momentarily. He reached for her again, burying his hands in her warm armpits. She had little tufts of red hair there and he allowed them to peak out between his

fingers as he drew her down to him so he could mouth
her breasts, which were large enough for him to
squeeze them together and suck on both nipples at the
same time.

"Oh, God," she said, "you show me something
new every time, something different. Ah, God, yes,
suck them, bite them. . . ."

She began to ride him up and down again as he
literally chewed her nipples, falling on him with all of
her weight when she came down so as to take him as
deeply inside as possible. When he came it was like an
unstoppable geyser shooting up inside of her, and that,
coupled with the dual manipulation of her large russet
nipples, seemed to trigger a climax twice as big as
before.

Still later she asked for something else new.

He told her to take him in her mouth and suck him,
and when he was slick with her saliva he directed her to
turn around on all fours and thrust her ass at him. He
parted her generous, white cheeks and probed her little
brown hole first with a moistened index finger, and
then with the head of his penis, sliding himself into her
gently, inch by inch, until his balls were banging
themselves against the backs of her thighs and the
lower portions of her cheeks.

When he came this time she clenched her powerful
muscles and he felt as if she were going to pull his cock
off as he erupted inside of her.

"Enough," he said later as her hand fell onto his limp
penis. "It's dead."

"It is not," she said, and as proof she fondled it until
it came semierect.

"See?"

"Well, then, it needs a rest."

"All right," she said, relenting. She put her head on his chest and said, "But not a very long rest."

"Just long enough," he said, but before he even finished her even breathing told him that she had fallen asleep.

Maybe it was the first peaceful sleep she'd had since she was seventeen.

He hoped it was.

TWENTY

Sometime later they were in the same position they were in that morning—eating together in the hotel dining room—only this time it was a late lunch.

The conversation had finally gotten around to John Titus, whom she had known as James Tillman.

"There's a kid around here who may be on his payroll," Clint told her. "Fancies himself handy with a gun."

"Is he?"

"He's killed a few men over the past month."

"What is he to you?"

"I'm looking for him, for a friend."

"A lady friend?"

He nodded. "His sister."

He told her about Sheena O'Shay and about Danny. He told her that he might have prevented the kid from becoming what he had become.

"You sound like me now," she said. "Aren't you the fella who told me I had no control over what happened to my family? Sounds like you ought to listen to your own words."

"Maybe you're right."

After a moment of silence she asked, "Do you think he'll send your O'Shay after me?"

"If he does," Clint answered, "I'll be there to stop him."

"Is that your plan?"

He shrugged and said, "It's as good as any. The only other thing I could do is go back to Titus's ranch and tear it apart looking for him."

"Maybe," Scarlet suggested, "he'll send O'Shay after you."

Clint was about to argue, but stopped short.

"What's wrong?" she asked.

"I hadn't considered that," he admitted. "If this kid is out to make himself a reputation—"

"Killing you would go a long way toward doing it."

"Right."

"Well, if he tries," she said, "I'll be there to stop him."

Clint and Scarlet were in her room when Frank Valin, Danny O'Shay, and three other men rode into town.

"What are we supposed to do?" one of the other men asked the foreman.

"Stay out of trouble," Valin said, "and be where I can find you if I need you."

"The saloon," one of the others said.

"That's fine," Valin said. "O'Shay, you stay with me."

"I want a drink."

Valin squinted at him and said, "You drink?"

"Sure."

"Okay, we'll get a drink," Valin said, "but you stay with me anyway."

They stopped in front of the saloon and as they were dismounting Valin said to one of the men, "Moss, you put the horses up at the livery."

Moss stopped short as he was in the act of dismounting, then climbed back in the saddle and accepted the reins of the other horses.

"Save me some whiskey."

"There'll be plenty." He turned to O'Shay and said, "O'Shay, come with me to the hotel."

"I want a drink," O'Shay said again.

"You'll get a drink, but first come with me to the hotel. We've got to check on something."

Reluctantly, O'Shay agreed, and followed Valin across the street to the hotel.

"Wait outside," the foreman instructed him, "and if you see Adams, don't do anything but say hello."

"If I see him—"

"Just say hello," Valin said again, and entered the lobby.

From where they were seated, Clint was able to see past Scarlet into the lobby.

"Hello," he said, and Scarlet turned. They both watched Frank Valin moving toward the desk, which was out of their sight. When they couldn't see him anymore she turned back to Clint and said, "That's Titus's foreman."

"He's not—"

"No," she said, shaking her head. "He's not one of the men I'm looking for."

"You may have to go through him to get to Titus, though," he said.

"That wouldn't be a problem," she assured him.

"You're a tough lady, aren't you?"

"Not tough," she corrected him. "I would prefer to be called determined."

"Did you ever consider giving it up, and going back to a normal life?"

"What's normal?" she asked.

They went back to their lunch.

Valin stopped at the desk and took a look at the register. When he didn't see the name he was looking for, he closed the book, pushed it back at the desk clerk, and went back outside.

When he saw Valin, Danny O'Shay pushed away from the wall he'd been leaning against with his arms folded. "Now can we get a drink?" he asked impatiently.

"Sure, kid," Valin said, patting O'Shay on one bony shoulder, "now we'll get a drink."

TWENTY-ONE

When Ross Bowman rode down Pleasant Point's main street he had already decided to shun the hotel in favor of a boardinghouse. Most towns had one of each.

He reined in his horse near a man crossing the street and called out, "Hey, old man."

The man looked up at him, squinting against the sun that seemed to have settled on his shoulder, and said, "Are you talking to me?"

"I don't see any other old men around."

"Wise youngster," the old man muttered, which amused the forty-three-year-old Bowman.

"This town got a boardinghouse?"

"Yeah," the old man said, "and it's got a hotel too."

"I'm only interested in the boardinghouse."

"Hotel's better," the old man warned.

"Old man," Bowman said, "point me in the direction of the boardinghouse—while you still can."

The old man pointed with a shaky finger toward the opposite end of town and said, "Ride to the end of the

113

street. It's a white frame house on the right."

"Thanks."

"No need to threaten old folks," the old man was muttering as Bowman rode away from him.

Bowman found the house, tied his horse off on the picket fence in front of it, and knocked on the door.

The woman who answered was in her early forties, with a slack mouth and heavy breasts. Sexy, in a worn out, slutty way, Bowman thought.

"Yeah?" she demanded.

"I'm looking for a room."

"What's the matter with the hotel?"

"It can't offer what you can," Bowman said, staring into the woman's lifeless eyes.

Her hand strayed up onto her cheek as she took a better look at him, then she said, "Yeah, okay, I got a room."

"Fine," he said. "I'll put my horse up at the livery and come back. You serve meals?"

"What's this look like, a restaurant?" she demanded. "I serve breakfast and dinner, and if you miss it, you miss it."

"Do I have time to make dinner?"

"You have time, big man," she said.

"Fine."

Bowman turned to walk away and the woman called out to him, "Hey, what's your name, big man?"

"Bowman."

"I'm Mrs. Gibson," she said, and then added, "Phyllis Gibson."

"Fine."

He turned to walk to his horse again and she called out, "Don't you wanna know how much I charge?"

He indicated that he didn't with a backward wave of his hand.

Bowman walked his horse into the livery and handed him over to the liveryman.

"Take good care of him," he said. Just because of the way the big gunman looked, the liveryman took that as a threat.

Moss, one of the Titus's hands, had finished taking care of the five horses he'd brought to the place and was on his way out when he spotted Bowman. He stared at the six-foot-five gaunt-faced man who wore a Navy Colt low on his left hip, said to himself, "Christ, that's Ross Bowman," and hurriedly left the livery for the saloon.

"Who are we waiting for?" Moss asked sometime later. He had been the last man to arrive at the saloon and had quickly made up for lost time.

"We're waiting," Valin said to him.

Moss squinted across the table at the foreman and repeated, "But for who?"

"Moss, why are you so interested?" Valin asked.

"Well," Moss said, "I saw a fella over in the livery that I don't want to see again, and sooner or later he's gonna come in here for a drink."

Valin ignored Moss but one of the other men, Bates, asked, "Who'd ya see, Moss?"

"You ain't gonna believe this," Moss said. "I didn't, but there he was, as big as life and twice as ugly—and he's got to be here for somebody, because his kind don't just ride through a town—"

"For chrissake, who was it?" Bates asked.

Moss hesitated for dramatic effect, then said, "Ross Bowman."

"Hell, you ain't ser—" Bates started to say, but Valin cut him off.

"You saw Ross Bowman?"

"Who's Ross Bowman?" Danny O'Shay asked.

"Well, yeah," Moss said, puzzled as to why the foreman seemed so riled.

"Why didn't you tell me before?"

"I didn't know," Moss said. "You mean we're sitting here waiting for Ross Bowman?"

"Who's Bowman?" O'Shay asked.

"Hey, a kid like you who thinks he's a gunny doesn't know who Ross Bowman is?" Bates asked.

"I never heard the name."

"You wouldn't have," Valin said. "He ain't as famous as the Gunsmith, but some say he's just as deadly."

"You mean, Mr. Titus sent for another gun when he had me all along?" O'Shay asked.

"Surprised he ain't sent for two," Bates said.

"Bates, if you wanna step outside—"

"Shut up, all of you," Valin snapped, then addressed himself to Moss: "Where'd he go?"

"I dunno," Moss replied drunkenly. "I got outta there real fast."

"I'll have to check the hotel again," Valin said, standing up.

"I'll come along," O'Shay said. "I want to meet this big gun—"

"No, you stay here," Valin said quickly, then added, "keep the boys here out of trouble."

"Him," Bates said as Valin strode toward the door, "keep us out of trouble?"

•   •   •

Valin checked the hotel again and was in the lobby checking the register as Clint and Scarlet came out of the dining room.

"Lose your job, Valin?" Clint asked.

"What makes you say that?"

"Checking in, aren't you?"

"No, I ain't checking in," Valin said. He pushed the register back at the clerk and left.

"What was that all about?" Scarlet wondered aloud.

"He was checking the register," Clint said, "and this is the second time. He's obviously in town waiting for someone."

"For who?" Scarlet asked.

"I guess that's what we'll have to find out."

TWENTY-TWO

Valin was halfway to the saloon when he remembered the boardinghouse. Sure, he thought, that's where Bowman must have gone. He probably wanted to stay away from the hotel. Valin changed direction and headed for the other end of town.

Clint Adams was far enough behind him not to be seen, close enough not to lose sight of him.

When Phyllis Gibson answered the door she recognized Valin from her days working at the Pleasant Point House of Paradise.

"Hello, Phyllis."

"What do you want?" she asked.

"Is that any way to treat an old friend?"

"Those days are over, Frank."

"Yeah," he said, taking in her appearance, "they sure are."

"What do you want?"

"I want to talk to one of your boarders."

"Who?"

"A man called Bowman."

119

She frowned and said, "How did you—"

"Then he's here?"

"He just got in today."

"Good," he said, trying to step by her.

She blocked his path and said, "I'll tell him you're here."

"All right, Phyllis," Valin said, although he knew he could have pushed by her. "I'll wait here."

She closed the door in his face and when it opened a few moments later he was looking at a big man wearing a gun on his left hip. He looked into the man's piercing eyes and gaunt face and knew why he had heard Titus refer to him as "Walking Death."

"You want me?"

"My name's Valin," the foreman said, annoyed with himself for becoming nervous in the presence of the gunman. "I'm the foreman out at the Big-T—"

"Titus's spread."

"That's right," Valin said. "I'm here in town to meet you."

"Well, you've met me," the man said, and started to close the door.

"Wait."

"What is it?"

"Aren't you going to come out to the ranch? Mr. Titus wants you—"

"Later," Bowman told the foreman. "Tell Titus I'll be out later."

"But Mr. Titus—"

"He'll wait," Bowman said, cutting Valin off. "Just tell him."

Bowman closed the door in Frank Valin's face.

● ● ●

"What did he want?" Phyllis Gibson asked Bowman as he walked into the sitting room.

"None of your business," Bowman said. "When will dinner be ready?"

"In about an hour. You can wait—"

"I have another appetite that needs taking care of in the meanwhile," Bowman said.

"I don't know what you—"

He reached out and grabbed Phyllis Gibson's left breast. It was firm and heavy and he squeezed it until the pain was etched on her face.

"Do you think you can help me?"

"Mister," she said, attempting to escape his grasp, "all you had to do was ask."

Clint had positioned himself across the street from the boardinghouse. From there he witnessed the exchange between Valin and the woman, and then when the big man came to the door, he'd recognized him immediately.

"Ross Bowman," he said to himself.

Bowman was one of those men who quietly went about his job, which was killing people. Only people who used him, made their way in this world with gun, or simply paid attention to such things as reputations, would have heard of him.

Clint felt that John Titus fit securely into the first category.

Valin returned to the saloon and told the men, "Let's go."

"What about Bowman?" O'Shay asked.

"Shut up!" Valin said. He was still seething from

the way Bowman had treated him, but he was even angrier that he hadn't been man enough to do something about it. "We're heading back for the ranch now," he told them all. "Anybody object?" When nobody did he said, "Then let's ride."

TWENTY-THREE

Clint found Scarlet waiting for him in his room, not hers, after checking hers first.

"You figured it out," he said, entering his room.

"Yes," she said, seated on the bed. On the chair by the window he saw her rifle and saddlebags.

She was a smart lady. She knew that Bowman had to be in town after her, so she'd moved her gear to Clint's room, in case Bowman made his move early.

"We've got some time," Clint assured her.

"How much?"

"He's got to go out and talk to Titus first. That gives us at least until tomorrow."

"Or tonight."

Clint shook his head.

"Bowman isn't the type to come after you at night, from a window."

"You sound like you know him."

"I know his type."

"You said 'we.' "

"What?"

"Before," she said. "You said, 'We've got some time.' What did you mean by 'we'?"

"We," he said again, "as in you and me. I can't leave—at least, not until I've seen or talked to Danny O'Shay. While I'm here I might as well lend you a hand."

"How about two?"

"What?"

"And a mouth," she went on, "and maybe a—"

"I get the picture," he said, his hands moving to the buttons on his shirt.

When Valin, O'Shay, and the others reached the ranch, Valin told them to get lost while he reported to Titus.

"I'll come too," O'Shay said.

"No, you won't," Valin said, turning to face him. The kid thought he was a hotshot gun, but that didn't scare Valin.

"You'll stay out here until Mr. Titus calls for you . . . if he calls for you."

Valin didn't wait to see what O'Shay's reaction would be. He turned and strode straight toward the house. He entered without knocking and started for Titus's office but stopped when he saw his boss coming downstairs.

"Valin? Did he get in?" Titus asked, peering past the foreman.

"Yes, sir."

"Where is he, in the office?" Titus asked. He came down the rest of the way and started for the office.

"Uh, no, he's not in there."

Titus stopped short and turned around.

"Well, then, where is he? In the saloon?"

"I left him at the boardinghouse," Valin said.

"Well, when is he coming out?"

"He didn't say, exactly . . . but he'll be out. He said he would—"

"I know he will," Titus said, relaxing. "Bowman's got a mind of his own, damn it."

"I can get some more of the men and go and get him—" Valin began.

"That'd be a foolish move, Frank," Titus said. "You'd all end up dead. He'll be out in his own time."

"That's it?" Valin asked. Although Titus had used Bowman before, Valin hadn't been around then. He didn't know that Titus and Bowman, because of their past, operated more or less on the same level.

"That's it," Titus said. "I'm going into my office to take care of some paperwork. Have a man watch for him and bring him to me as soon as he rides in."

"Yes, sir."

As Titus turned to walk away Valin said, "Boss?"

"Yeah?"

"O'Shay's getting impatient."

"Keep him in line," Titus said, walking away. When he reached the door to his office he turned and said, "You can do that, can't you?"

"Sure."

"You know," Titus said, this time with the door open and his hand on the knob, "if I know Bowman, he's snuggled up somewhere with something soft."

"He didn't go near the saloon," Valin said, "or the whorehouse."

Titus grinned, shook his head, and stepped into his office, closing the door behind him, and Valin remembered that Phyllis ran the boardinghouse.

But Phyllis wasn't in the business anymore.

Was she?

"You're rough," Phyllis Gibson said, but even though she was lying on her bed with bruises on both breasts, she wasn't complaining.

She was stating fact.

Bowman was getting dressed. He strapped on his gun before answering. "You enjoyed it."

"I—" she started, as if she were going to complain, but she stopped short because she couldn't deny it. She knew it, and Bowman knew it. The way she'd raked his back during her orgasm had nothing to do with trying to get him off her—if anything, she'd been trying to take him deeper inside.

"If we don't try to kid each other," Bowman said, "my visit here might be pleasant—for both of us."

"Where are you going?"

"I've got someone to see, but I'll be back," Bowman assured her. "Keep it warm for me."

He left and Phyllis rubbed her sore breasts lightly. She'd never known a man before who could hurt her and make it feel good.

TWENTY-FOUR

Ross Bowman rode up to John Titus's house and turned his horse over to a ranch hand who seemed to be waiting for him.

"You Bowman?"

"That's right."

"Wait right here, then," the man said. "I'll get the foreman and he'll take you in—"

"I don't need the foreman," Bowman said. "I'll find my own way in."

"Hey—" the man said, but Bowman brushed past him and entered the house. He thought a moment, remembered where the office was, and walked to it.

As he walked in Titus looked up, frowning until he recognized him.

"Bowman."

The gunman shut the door behind him and said, "Hello, John. Got another problem you can't handle yourself, huh?"

"It's not that," Titus said, going on the defensive immediately. That seemed to be the way Bowman always affected him. "It's just that this particular problem needs your special touch. On top of that, you'll have a special interest in this one.''

"I don't get personally involved in my jobs, John," Bowman said. "You know that." He took a seat. "Tell me about it, John."

"It goes back a few years, to a young girl with red hair. Remember?"

"I remember," Bowman said, and Titus thought the man's face seemed stiffer than when he came in. "She's here?"

"She's in town," Titus said, "and I think we can be sure she's after me."

"You want me to take care of her?"

"Remember one thing," Titus said. "She's already killed two of us—"

"Rumors."

"Maybe," Titus said, "but two of us are dead, and after me comes you and Griffin."

"Or maybe Griffin and then me."

"Either way, she'll get to you soon enough."

"Have you seen her?"

"No."

"Then maybe you're getting nervous for nothing, Titus," Bowman said.

"All right, since you're here already, take a look and tell me what you think."

Bowman hesitated, then said, "All right, but if it is her and I decide to do it, the price is still the same."

"You've got just as much at stake here as I do, Bowman," Titus said. "I'd think you'd do it for nothing."

Bowman leaned forward and said, "I could always wait for her to get past you and Griffin and *then* do it for nothing. I'd have an even bigger stake then, wouldn't I?''

"All right," Titus said, without hesitating. "Same price."

Bowman got up and said, "I'll take a look and get back to you."

"Make it soon, Bowman."

"It'll be tomorrow, don't worry," Bowman said. "I don't like to stay in one place too long. I'm not like you, Titus. I don't like to push my luck."

The reference was to Titus changing his name and putting down roots in one place—and then deciding to get into politics. Bowman and the other three hadn't gotten into anything that permanent.

"There's one other thing you should know before you leave," Titus said as Bowman walked toward the door.

"What's that?"

"Clint Adams is in town too."

"The Gunsmith?" Bowman said, frowning. "What's he got to do with this?"

"I don't know," Titus said. "All I know is that he's here and he wouldn't hire."

"You offered him the job?"

"I thought—"

"That was a fool move, Titus," Bowman said. "Adams doesn't hire out his gun."

"So he told me."

"Did you tell him who—"

"I didn't mention the girl, but he's been seen with her in town."

Titus saw a funny look come over Bowman's face and wondered what was going on in the other man's head. He didn't have long to wonder.

"If I were to kill the Gunsmith," Bowman said, as if he were talking to himself, "that'd boost my reputation higher than anybody's."

"The Gunsmith might not be involved—"

"That doesn't matter," Bowman said. "If it's the same girl, I'll take care of her for the same price, Titus, but the Gunsmith—I'll take care of him for personal reasons."

As Bowman walked out, Titus hoped he would at least wait until the girl was dead before he tried for the Gunsmith.

Just in case.

Bowman had his mind on only one thing during the ride back to town.

Clint Adams, the Gunsmith.

Oh, he knew that if the girl in town was the same girl, she would have to be his number one priority. . . .

Or would she?

He remembered what he had said to Titus just moments before. He could let the girl kill Titus and Griffin and wait for her to find him. She'd always come looking for him, so why take a chance now, a chance on losing the Gunsmith?

He decided that he'd make a try for the girl first, but if it went wrong, he was going after the Gunsmith. Once he had Clint Adam's name on his list, it would be real easy for the girl to find him after she killed the other two. All she'd have to do was follow his rep.

And he'd be waiting for her.

TWENTY-FIVE

Clint didn't know if Scarlet's hunger was for sex or for him. He gave her the benefit of the doubt and figured it was a little bit of both. Either way it went, he didn't really mind. She was a special kind of woman, and her kind didn't come along very often. He'd known some other special women—in fact, Scarlet reminded him a bit of both Lacy Blake* and Anne Archer,† both of whom were bounty hunters and, in a way, so was Scarlet.

"What are you thinking about?" she asked him. It was his first indication that she was awake after he'd given her both hands and much more, as she had requested.

"You," he said as she began to rub the palm of her hand over his chest. He didn't bother to tell her that he was comparing her to two women from his past. He

---

*The Gunsmith #24: Killer Grissly.
†The Gunsmith #35: The Bounty Women.

didn't think that it would appease her at all to find out that she had fared very well in the comparison.

"And what else?"

She persisted, so now he'd have to lie. "I was thinking about Titus and Bowman."

"Is Bowman . . . very good with a gun?"

"He's one of the best."

"Better than you?"

"I've never had an opportunity to find out," he replied, "and I'm not looking forward to it."

"What do you propose we do then," she asked, "leave? As long as we stay we know that he'll come after me, unless you intend—"

"I said I wasn't looking forward to the confrontation," Clint said, cutting her off. "I didn't say I'd back away from it. And to answer your question, no, I don't intend to let you face him. You might be good, but I don't know if you're that good."

"I don't know either," she said, surprising him with her frankness.

"The two men you killed, were they handy with a gun?" he asked.

"No, not very."

"Then you've never been severely tested, have you?"

She hesitated a moment, then said, "No, but then I never claimed to be a gunman."

"Gunlady."

"Whatever. What I am is determined, and if I had, have, to face Bowman to get to Titus, I will."

"You won't have to."

"I can't ask you to—"

"We'll try going around Bowman for the time being,'' Clint said. ''If that doesn't work then you won't have to ask me to face Bowman. I will . . . and you can have Titus. Is that good enough?''

''That's better than good,'' she said, snuggling close to him, ''and more than I would have asked.''

''Well, for a pretty lady I'm always ready to do more than I'm asked to do.''

''Really?'' she asked, reaching beneath the sheet. ''How much more?''

''I guess we'll see,'' he answered, running his hand over her breasts, ''won't we?''

He leaned over to run his tongue over her already hardening nipples, and she closed her hand around his stiffening shaft.

When Bowman returned to the boardinghouse, all the other boarders were either in their rooms or out seeking some sort of entertainment. Bowman, excited over the prospect of killing the Gunsmith, immediately searched for Phyllis and found her . . . in his room.

''Well,'' he said, closing the door behind him.

''I waited for you,'' she said, sitting up in bed. She had been asleep and his entry awakened her. As she sat up the sheet fell away, revealing her large, pendulous, and bruised breasts.

''What if I don't feel like having you now?'' he asked, unbuckling his gunbelt.

''Having me—'' she started, but then stopped as she remembered how his hands could hurt—really hurt!

''Then I'll go,'' she said, throwing the sheet off her totally and swinging her feet around to the floor.

''Never mind,'' he said, pulling his shirt out of his

pants and unbuttoning it. "Stay where you are. As it happens, I do feel like it."

Actually, she didn't really care. Ever since the first time he'd laid his hands on her she knew that she needed him to touch her again, even if it hurt . . . at first.

He approached the bed and wasted no time in mounting her. With no thought at all for her pleasure, he began to pound into her ruthlessly, paying no heed to her cries, whether they were of pleasure or of pain, thinking only of what it would be like when his gun went off and the first bullet punched its way into Clint Adams's body. He sought only his own release and when it came he groaned aloud, deaf to *her* cries of pleasure, and began to fill her as he had never filled a woman before.

Take that, Gunsmith!

In another part of town the coupling of man and woman was done with tenderness rather than brutality, with each party as eager for their partner's pleasure as they were for their own.

Just moments earlier Clint's searching, eager tongue had plumbed Scarlet's depths, setting her hips and buttocks to twitching and bouncing as she experienced another shattering climax.

"Oh, God!" Scarlet shouted, reaching for Clint eagerly with both hands. He gave her a last loving flick of his tongue and then crawled into her warm embrace, piercing her sweetly, throbbing inside of her.

"Yes," she whispered, and now he was plunging into her and she was holding him tightly with her arms and legs and moaning into his mouth.

"Clint," she breathed, pulling her mouth less than an inch from his.

"What?"

"I don't want you to get killed," she said, gasping as he continued to drive into her. "You can . . . uh . . . leave town tomorrow . . . I won't—"

"Scarlet."

"What?"

"You talk too much," he said with his lips on her neck. "Shut up."

She began to moan again as she felt him swell inside of her, and as he came it triggered another orgasm in her. Using her hands she grabbed his head and pulled his down so she could kiss him . . . and muffle her screams with his mouth.

"So what are we going to do?" Scarlet asked him sometime later.

"What we should do now is get out of this bed and get something to eat."

"It's late."

"Well," he said, looking at her, "we can get something to drink and talk about it over at the saloon."

"Talk about what we're going to do next?" she asked, getting up to get dressed.

"No," he said, studying the line of her bare back with great interest and appreciation—he liked the way it traveled into the crease between her firm buttocks—"talk about where we can get something to eat."

"I'm serious, Clint."

Clint leaned over, slapped her on the right cheek hard enough to leave a red imprint of his hand. She shrieked and jumped.

"So am I."

Bowman fucked Phyllis Gibson every way he knew how and finally got her down on all fours so he could take her from behind. It was nothing new to her, she had done worse when she was a working girl. What worried her was that she had never enjoyed it. She was enjoying it now . . . physically.

Mentally, she was cursing the big man out because he was undoing everything she'd done since she had left the Pleasant Point House of Paradise. She'd suppressed urges to go back over the past two years since taking over the boardinghouse, and he was bringing all of those urges back.

What would happen when he wasn't around to satisfy them? She'd end up whoring again to try and find a man who could.

He came and she closed her eyes, but there was no escaping the orgasm that shook her to her heels.

He withdrew from her, pushed her away, and got up from the bed. He washed himself off in a basin and then dressed, all while she watched him. She hated him with her eyes and lusted for him with her body. She was amazed that his cock was still semierect even after everything he'd done to her.

But why not? After all that, she still could have taken more from him.

"Where are you going?"

"Out, for a drink," he said, buckling his gunbelt.

"I have a bottle—"

"And some air."

"Would you like me to wait?"

He looked at her and left without answering.

"Sonofabitch!" she said, touching herself with her hands.

That old fire was lit again, and she hated it.

She decided to wait.

TWENTY-SIX

They went over to the saloon and Scarlet charmed
the bartender into rustling up a couple of cold chicken
sandwiches for them.

"You can be quite a charmer when you have to be,
can't you?" Clint asked as they took their sandwiches
and a couple of beers to a corner table.

"When I'm hungry I can charm a rattler out of his
skin," she said, smiling.

"You're in the wrong business, then," he said.
"You should be working as a con woman."

"You really think so?" she asked, arching her eye-
brows. "I'll think about it."

They were halfway through their sandwiches when
Ross Bowman walked through the batwing doors.
Scarlet's back was to the doors, but Clint saw him
immediately.

"What is it?" she asked, seeing the look in his face.

"Don't turn around," he said. "Ross Bowman just
walked in."

"Where?"

"He's going to the bar."

She turned in time to see his back, and couldn't see his reflection in the bar mirror clearly.

"Does he know you?"

"Oh yeah," Clint said, popping the last piece of bread into his mouth. "He spotted me the minute he walked in."

"How could you tell?"

He smiled and said, "He started salivating."

She grinned then and said, "Oh, yeah? Then he must have seen me too."

Bowman stood at the bar trying to catch a look at the redhead's face through the mirror. Christ, he thought, the hair's the right color and the body—she had a nice little body back then, but if this was her, look at her now.

He remembered that he'd been the first one, and she'd screamed when he popped her cherry. Smiling to himself, he remembered that she'd screamed even more as he kept going at her until he popped too.

The girl at the table turned her head at that moment, real quick, but Ross Bowman had quick eyes.

Damned if that ain't her, he thought. Wonder what she'd be like now?

Maybe he'd get a chance to find out . . . before he killed her.

"That's twice," Clint said.

"What do you mean?"

"That's twice you looked over at him," he said. "Don't do it again."

"Sorry."

"Don't be."

"What'd you mean when you said he was salivating?" she asked, eyeing him curiously.

"Oh, it's something you carry around with you when you've got a reputation," he explained. "Every little gun and big gun salivates when they think about that reputation hanging around their necks."

"You think he'll make a play for you because of your rep?"

"Oh, he wouldn't miss the chance, Scarlet, don't think twice about that," he said, swirling the remnants of his beer at the bottom of his mug. "Why, I can even tell you how he'll play it."

They both waited a couple of beats and then she gave in first. "How?"

"He'll try for you, first," he began, "and when he can't get to you—"

"Let's hope."

"—then he'll decide to go for me and to hell with Titus."

"He'll pass up whatever Titus is paying him for a chance at you?"

"Hell, yes."

"But nobody will ever hire him again."

"Yeah, but he'll have my rep."

"You think a lot of that reputation, don't you?" she asked.

"No," he answered, "but everybody else does."

And there *he* was, Bowman thought, in all his glory.

The Gunsmith.

The Legend.

The man everybody said was the fastest and the best, now that Hickok was gone.

Well, Bowman thought, allowing himself a small smile, that'll change.

He tossed off his whiskey, turned to leave, and caught the Gunsmith's eye. Not normally a demonstrative man, Bowman couldn't resist giving the man just a hint of a nod.

Which the Gunsmith returned.

He's got sharp eyes, the gunman thought as he walked out. I wonder how sharp his hands really are.

"What was that?"

"What was what?" Clint asked.

"You nodded," she said, then turned in time to see Bowman go out the door.

"He nodded, so I nodded."

"But that means—"

"That means he knows I'm here and I know he's here, and he knows that I know—" Clint stopped and shook his head. "Let's just say the fat's in the fire now, honey."

TWENTY-SEVEN

Danny O'Shay was sitting outside the bunkhouse, twirling his Colt, when two of the hands, Moss and Bates, came out and stared at him, at each other—a small nod between them—and then back at O'Shay.

"What's eating at you, O'Shay?" Moss asked. "You mad 'cause you ain't killed anybody lately?"

Moss was kidding, laughing as he asked it, but O'Shay's answer was dead serious.

"You can't make a reputation for yourself if you ain't killed anybody."

Moss and Bates exchanged glances again and then Moss said, "Well, boy, if that's the case, there's three ways you could go about fixing that."

"How?"

"Well, there's always Ross Bowman."

"Bowman?"

"Sure, you could go into town and call him out," Moss said, rubbing his jaw. "Of course, he's here to do a job for the boss."

"Well, so am I."

"Well, then you've got your pick of two," Moss

said. "You could call out the Gunsmith himself, or you could go to town and face that red-haired gal."

"What gal?"

"Well, you ain't heard this," Moss said, leaning over, "but we have, seeing as how we're pretty close to Valin, you know."

"So?" O'Shay demanded, squinting up at them. Bates was just standing by, grinning from ear to ear.

"So, Mr. Titus has got it in for that red-haired gal. Seems she's got a little bit of a reputation herself."

"With a gun?"

"That's what I hear."

"What's her name?" O'Shay asked eagerly. "Maybe I heard of her."

"Well, I heard somebody in town say she was called Scarlet."

O'Shay thought about that and then said with disappointment, "I never heard of her."

"Well, that don't mean she don't have a rep," Bates said, speaking for the first time. "For instance, we never heard of you, and you claim to have a rep."

"I do!" O'Shay said, standing up. "And pretty soon you and a lot of people will be hearing the name Danny O'Shay."

With that O'Shay turned on his heel and walked away from them and the bunkhouse.

"Now which one you figure he's gonna go after?" Valin asked later.

It had been Titus's idea to have some of the hands prod O'Shay into facing any of the three—Scarlet, Bowman or the Gunsmith.

"O'Shay might become a problem," Titus had said, "doing something on his own before we're ready.

Maybe now's the time to either make use of him or get rid of him.''

Moss told Valin, "I don't know, but I hope it's the girl.''

"Why's that?''

"Well, because if it's Bowman or the Gunsmith, I don't think he's gonna get much further.''

"Well," Valin said, shaking his head, "that'd be too bad, wouldn't it?''

O'Shay walked a short distance from the ranch buildings and then stopped to think. It's only right for a man to work his way up, he thought. Surely nobody could blame him for that.

That meant starting with the red-haired woman and then moving on to either Bowman or Adams. Of course, waiting for those two to face each other could also work. He could kill the winner and end up with both their reps hanging from his belt.

Hell, it'd also be fun to watch.

Bowman and the Gunsmith.

O'Shay wondered which one would win.

Ross Bowman went back to the rooming house and found Phyllis Gibson asleep in his bed. She had an appetite, that one, he thought while looking down at her. It was like she wanted him to do the things he did to her. Like she hated them and enjoyed them at the same time.

Well, he sure enjoyed doing them to her.

She was sprawled across the bed on her stomach, the sheet tangled around her ankles. He examined her critically, noting that her behind was big and her thighs heavy. He walked over and ran his hand over the curve of one meaty cheek and she turned onto her back, as if to aid him in his examination. Her breasts, flattened out against her chest, were certainly large, but they weren't as firm as they had probably once been. He touched one nipple and it tightened immediately. Her belly was rounded, not flat the way most young women today liked them to be.

And she certainly wasn't young. . . .

It's a good thing I like my women meaty, he thought, his penis beginning to swell, because she sure fits that description. Unbuckling his gunbelt, he started to put it down and then paused. He slid it out of the holster and hefted it.

He was thinking about putting one in the Gunsmith's belly while "the Legend" gaped at him, Adams's gun still in his holster because he hadn't been fast enough to get it out against Ross Bowman.

That made Bowman's penis swell even more.

TWENTY-EIGHT

Clint and Scarlet spent the night in his room without bothering to check her out of hers. Clint still doubted that Bowman would make a try for her during the night, but they both thought that playing it safe was the best way.

It was also more fun.

If she *hadn't* slept in his bed, she wouldn't be waking him up now by running her tongue over his chest, teasing his nipples, moving down across the expanse of his stomach, probing his navel, washing over his thighs and hips, and finally laving his balls and penis, sucking him to fullness.

"Good morning to you too," he said. She looked up at him from her position between his legs, grinned, and then immediately went back to work on him, taking him into her mouth. He moved one leg beneath her so that her nipples were brushing his thigh. In reply she reached up and cupped his sac and began to suck on him in earnest.

"Scarlet—" he said as he felt the familiar rush building up inside of him.

147

"Mmmm," she replied, or it may have just been a moan of pleasure.

He reached down to cup her head in his hands and began to do some moaning of his own. For someone who had always thought that this act was demeaning to a woman, she was doing one hell of a job on him. He thought she might simply be building him to the breaking point, at which point she'd mount him, but it soon became apparent that she was intent on sucking him to completion.

He didn't want that. He wanted to be inside her, stoking her fire as she was stoking his.

"Scarlet," he said, trying to pull her head away, but she resisted.

He tried again.

"Scarlet, I want to be inside of you," he said, pulling on her head. Her head began to shake and he soon realized that she was laughing. She had to release *him* in order to release the laugh and that's when he pulled her on top of him.

"What are you laughing at?" he demanded.

"You," she said. "You sounded so serious."

"I am," he said. He took her by the hips and maneuvered her so that the head of his engorged penis was positioned right against the slick lips of her pussy.

"Um," she said, "yes," and as she said yes he entered her, swiftly and cleanly.

Her mouth quickly latched onto his and as his penis drove in and out of her, her tongue drove in and out of him. Finally he closed his teeth on her tongue, chewing gently, and kneaded her buttocks while he plowed her furrow.

"Yes," she murmured against his mouth as she felt her climax approaching, and then "Oh, yes!" as it built, and then "God, Jesus, Clint," as if the three formed some sort of trinity. "Yes, that's it, that's wonderful, that's delicious," and then she was bouncing up and down on him wordlessly, the only sounds from her mouth resembling tortured moans, although he knew they were moans of pure unbridled pleasure.

And then he exploded inside of her. . . .

"What's our first move of the day?" she asked later.

"Hmm?" he said without opening his eyes. "I thought we just had—"

"All right," she said, raising herself up on one elbow so she could look down at him. "What's our second move of the day, then?"

"Ah," he said, opening first one eye and then the other, "I think we should get dressed, have breakfast, and then take a ride out to Titus's land."

"His land?" she asked, frowning. "What for?"

"To see if he's set up any kind of security to keep you out," he explained. "I'm sure you wouldn't be able to just ride up to his house the way I did without getting shot at, but let's see how close we can get, huh?"

"I'm with you," she said. They stared at each other for a few seconds and then she lowered her head so she could use the tip of her tongue to outline his mouth. He opened his mouth then, she plunged her tongue into it, and they engaged in a long, deep kiss, as if each were testing the other's ability to go without air.

"Mmm," he said, finally breaking the kiss, "I'm hungry."

"For?"

"Food."

"Oh," she said, feigning a look of disappointment.

"How about getting up and letting me watch you get dressed?" he asked.

"Why?"

"Because you're beautiful and I want to watch you."

"You'll make me nervous."

"Getting dressed?"

"I'll trip on my pants."

"You won't."

"I'll drop my gun and shoot myself."

"No, you won't."

"I'll—"

"You won't."

She stared at him, then said, "Oh, all right. Watch."

She leaped out of bed and he watched her breasts jiggle and bounce as she collected her clothes and climbed into them. She did almost fall once, while pulling her boots on, and finally sat on the bed to do it. Lastly, she buckled her gunbelt, then executed a curtsy, indicating that the show was over.

"You're beautiful," he said, and then got up to dress while she watched.

"So are you."

"No argument," he said. "Now that that's settled, let's go and eat."

After breakfast they went to the livery to saddle their horses. When Scarlet laid eyes on Duke, her mouth formed an *O* of wonderment.

"He's magnificent," she gushed, walking around the big black gelding.

"Not so loud," Clint said, lifting his saddle onto Duke's broad back, "you'll turn his head."

At that point Duke turned his head to look at Scarlet

and Clint said, "See? Lucky for you he's a gelding."

She made a face at him and said, "He looks like he understands everything we're saying."

"He does."

She walked to her own bay and began to saddle her.

"I haven't named her," she admitted.

"Why not?"

"I had a horse shot out from under me once, and since then I try not to get too attached to any of my mounts."

"Including me?"

"Well," she said, "there are exceptions."

As she mentioned having a horse shot out from beneath her, Clint couldn't help but remember the one time that Duke had been shot and almost died.* He knew the time would come when Duke would no longer be around, but then he knew that time would come for him, too, and there was nothing he could do in either case, so he simply tried not to dwell on it.

When they were saddled, they mounted up and walked the horses outside.

"Before we start, I want to get something straight."

"What?"

"We're treating this as a recon mission only. We're not going out there to take anybody on. Understand?"

"I understand."

"Put more plainly," he said, "if anybody starts shooting, we start running. Got it?"

"Perfectly."

"All right, then let's ride."

They mounted up and proceeded out of town, passing the boardinghouse on the way.

---

*The Gunsmith #31: Trouble Rides a Fast Horse.

TWENTY-NINE

Ross Bowman was looking out his window as Clint Adams and the woman passed. He watched them ride out of town and assumed they were going out to check Titus's security. He hoped it wasn't too good. He didn't want the Gunsmith being shot down by a bunch of quick-triggered cow punchers.

"Bowman?" Phyllis called from the bed behind him.

"What?"

"Do you want breakfast?"

"In a little while," he replied, turning away from the table to look at her. "Right now the only breakfast I want is between your legs, woman."

"I've got to make breakfast for the others—" she started to protest.

He gave her a hard stare, and said, "To hell with the others." Approaching the bed and towering over her, he commanded, "Spread your legs."

She made an attempt to match his stare but quickly averted her eyes and obediently spread her meaty thighs with a mixture of dread and excitement. When

153

his head was buried there and she could feel his tongue beginning to dart around inside her, she came immediately, shuddering.

That had never happened before. In fact, she had never come as quickly or as often with any man before, and she wondered idly if a woman could die from this.

Bowman seemed determined to answer that question right there and then, for in spite of her massive climax, he continued to use his tongue to manipulate her clit, bringing her to a second, almost painful climax.

"Bowman—" she said, starting to sit up.

"Shut up," he said, putting his hand on her large breasts and pushing her back down. His erection was huge, prodding at the air like a beast seeking release, and he climbed atop her and brutally rammed it into her.

"Bowman," she cried out, and it was at once a cry of delight and a plea for mercy.

Bowman reached beneath her to cup her generous buttocks and began to manipulate her that way, both slamming into her and pulling her against him. He was gripping her flesh so tightly that even he felt the pressure in his fingers.

"Bow-man," she moaned, her eyes rolling up to look at the ceiling, threatening to roll up into her head as everything began to whirl around her.

She knew that this vicious man had given her more pleasure during the last couple of days than she had ever realized during all her years as a whore, but she also knew that too much of anything was dangerous.

God, she thought, as a third orgasm roared inside of her, I *am* going to die.

Minutes later she realized that Bowman was no longer atop her and she hadn't died. She sat up, looked around her, and saw that he was bent over a basin of water, dousing his face and torso. He grabbed a towel, turned around while drying his chest, and stopped when he saw her.

"Aren't you getting breakfast yet?"

Not sure she could stand on her shaky legs, she nevertheless moved to the edge of the bed to try.

"I'll get it now."

"Well, hurry up."

She stood up, unsteadily at first and then, with more control, began to dress.

"All right," John Titus said, addressing the assemblage of men in front of his house. "You all know where you're supposed to be and who you're supposed to stop."

"Yes, sir," Valin answered for all of them.

"If the Gunsmith shows, I don't want anyone getting killed trying to trade shots with him."

"Sir?" one of the men called out.

"Yes," Titus said, frowning. He could not think of the man's name.

"What about Barrow hands?"

"Good question," Titus said to the man, and then again addressed the rest of them. "Any Barrow hand is to be left alone. I want your minds on only one person—the woman who calls herself Scarlet. If she trespasses on my land, I want you to bring her to me."

There was a chorus of "yessirs," then Titus dismissed them. As they dispersed and went to get their horses, Valin mounted the front steps to speak to Titus.

"Are your men set?" Titus asked.

"Yes, sir. Moss, Zeke, and some of the others know what they're supposed to do," Valin said. "She'll be

shot on sight because they know you'll stand behind
their story."

"Fine, fine," Titus said. "Valin, I don't want her
getting anywhere near this house. We'll keep her away
until Bowman does his job."

"Yes, sir."

"Where's O'Shay?" Titus asked. "I didn't see him
here."

Valin looked uncomfortable.

"Valin?"

"He's gone, Mr. Titus."

"Gone?"

"Took off during the night, I guess."

"Let's hope whatever he does is in our best interest," Titus said.

"I hope so, sir."

"Although I would have liked it better if we could
have kept an eye on him. If you see him . . ."

"Yes sir?"

Titus thought for a moment, then said, "Ah, hell, if
you see him tell him, I want the Gunsmith dead. That
ought to take care of one of them."

"O'Shay, I'd think."

"Well, Bowman can have Adams after he's taken
care of Scarlet. I'm sure he'll like that. All those
reputation seekers are the same."

"Yes, sir."

"You'd better get along with the rest of them, Valin."

"I've left enough men to keep you and the house
covered, sir."

"Thank you, Valin," Titus said. "When this is all
over, I'll see to it that you're rewarded for standing by
me."

"Just doing my job, sir," Valin said, but when he turned his back on Titus to descend the steps, a tight grin formed.

He hoped the reward would be in cash.

From a safe vantage point Danny O'Shay watched John Titus's men disperse and set out for the four corners of the Titus ranch. From there they would patrol as much of the land as they could, hoping to keep the woman, Scarlet, away from their boss.

O'Shay was determined to accomplish the same thing but in his own way. He was going to go to town and gun down this red-haired woman Titus was so scared of, then present himself to Titus for a proper reward.

After that, it would be either Bowman or Clint Adams. He felt a moment's regret about the Gunsmith being killed, but decided it served Adams right. He refused to help O'Shay when he asked him to and now the would-be student might end up killing the would-be teacher.

Oh, well, he thought, mounting his horse and preparing to ride for town, the old have to make way for the new, and Danny O'Shay's career was just beginning.

THIRTY

It didn't take Clint Adams and Scarlet long to discover what Titus had done.

"He's blanketed his property with men," Clint said.

They were sitting atop a rise near a cluster of trees looking down at a group of three men who were riding by. It was the fourth such grouping they'd seen in the past half hour, and it had only been luck that they had avoided confrontations with any of them.

"Looks like Titus is a little concerned about me," Scarlet commented.

"Concerned . . . or scared."

"Well, either way, I'm glad he's thinking about me."

"He probably figures to try and keep you away from the house until Bowman does his job."

"How are we going to get to him with all these men around?"

"We can't, there's too many of them."

"What can we do then?"

Clint looked at Scarlet and said, "Maybe we can make him come to us."

159

"You're willing to draw him to me so I can kill him?"

"I don't expect you to gun him down in cold blood."

She stiffened and said, "The others had a fair chance, Clint, and so will Titus."

"All right, then let's get back to town and see what we can do."

"What *are* we going to do?"

"I don't know," Clint said, "but maybe I can think of something on the way."

When they reached town, they went to the livery to put up their horses and Scarlet asked, "Well?"

"Well what?"

"Did you get any ideas?"

"One."

"You going to tell me about it?"

"Sure," he said, lifting the saddle off Duke's back. "Let's go and talk to the law."

Sheriff Resnick's first reaction when Clint and Scarlet entered his office was to gape at the red-haired woman, mouth open.

"Close your mouth, Sheriff, before something flies in," Clint suggested.

The man's mouth snapped shut and he gave the Gunsmith an annoyed look.

"What do you want, Adams?"

"Just to have a talk."

"About what?"

"Not what," Scarlet said. "Who."

"All right, lady," Resnick said, trying to keep a tremor out of his voice, "who?"

"John Titus," she said.

"One of our leading citizens?"

"Who doesn't like him?" Clint asked.

"What do you mean by that?"

"Just what I said. Who doesn't like him?"

"I don't know," Resnick complained. "He's a big man in this town—"

"Which means there's got to be somebody who doesn't like him," Scarlet said, cutting the man off. "All we want is one name, Sheriff."

Resnick looked as if he had just bit into something sour, then said, "All right, I suppose you could find this out on the street. Titus and Victor Barrow don't get along at all."

"And where do we find Victor Barrow?"

"Probably at the bank at this time of day. I saw him in town earlier."

"Where would he normally be?"

"On his ranch," Resnick said. "He used to have the biggest spread in these parts, until Titus showed up and started to, ah, acquire land."

"You saying that Barrow is jealous of Titus?"

"It's more than that," the lawman said. "Those two just naturally don't like each other, like a dog and a cat. Barrow thinks that Titus's methods are—"

"Illegal?" Scarlet asked.

" 'Distasteful,' he says," Resnick answered.

"Thanks for your help, Sheriff."

"This, uh, won't find its way back to Mr. Titus, will it?" the sheriff asked, nervously.

"Like you said, Sheriff," Clint said, opening the door for Scarlet, "I could have gotten it from anybody on the street."

●   ●   ●

"Uh, can I help you, sir?" the young teller asked, staring past Clint at Scarlet.

"I'm looking for Victor Barrow. I understand he came in here not long ago."

"Mr. Barrow?"

Clint deliberately stepped in front of the man, obstructing his view of Scarlet, and said, "That's right, Victor Barrow."

"Oh, yes, Mr. Barrow," the teller said, "I, uh, think he's in with Mr. Garvin."

"Who's Mr. Garvin?"

"George Garvin," the teller said, indicating a door behind him. A plate on the door said, GEORGE GARVIN, BANK PRESIDENT.

"I'd like to see him, please."

"Mr. Garvin?"

"Mr. Barrow."

"I'll see if he's there," the teller said. He snuck one more look at Scarlet, then turned, knocked on the door, and entered. A few moments later he came out and walked back behind his cage.

"I'm afraid Mr. Barrow and Mr. Garvin are busy right now."

"When won't they be busy?"

"Uh, they didn't say . . . sir."

"All right, never mind," Clint said. He turned and called out, "Scarlet," then started around the cage with her following.

"Uh, sir, I'm sorry," the teller said nervously, his voice rising a couple of octaves, "you can't come behind the cage. Uh, miss—"

"Don't worry, friend," Scarlet told him, chucking him under the chin, "we'll make sure he knows you told us."

Clint opened the door without knocking and walked in. There was one man seated behind a desk and one in front. The Gunsmith was no detective but he figured that the one in front must be Barrow.

"Mr. Barrow?"

The man behind the desk—George Garvin, no doubt—stood up to his full five-foot-six and bellowed, "What's the meaning of this?"

Garvin was a small man, but his voice was big and loud. It was probably his best weapon, and he knew how to use it. He was in his late fifties, with a gray mustache and gray hair on either side of a bald pate.

"Sorry to break in on your meeting, gentlemen, but I'd like to talk to Mr. Barrow," Clint said. "I'll try not to take up too much of his time."

Behind him he heard Scarlet close the door. Both men looked past him—the seated Barrow craning his neck—and stared at her. She smiled and stared back.

"Hello, gentlemen."

"Are you with this man?" Garvin demanded.

"All the way."

"George," Barrow said, "let's see what these determined people want."

Barrow stood up to his full height of a somewhat emaciated six-three. He was in his early sixties but despite this, his thinning hair—which came to a widow's peak—was brown without a trace of gray. Clint wondered idly if he was vain enough to color his hair, as he knew some women did.

"What is it you want to see me about?"

"John Titus."

"Are you friends of John Titus?" Barrow asked, his distaste for the man plainly written across his angular face.

"Not even close," Scarlet said, matching Barrow's dislike.

"Like the lady says," Clint said, "we're definitely not friends of John Titus."

"George," Barrow said, looking at Garvin, "get these nice people a drink."

THIRTY-ONE

After George Garvin had given them each a glass of brandy, Clint made the introductions.

"My name is Clint Adams and this lady is Scarlet."

"Just Scarlet?" Barrow asked.

"It'll do," she answered.

"What have you got to tell us about John Titus?" Garvin asked.

"A way to bring him down, if you're interested," Clint said.

"We are!" Garvin said, and Clint got the impression that the bank president was even more anxious than Barrow.

"What about you, Mr. Barrow?" Clint asked. "I've heard you don't like Titus."

"I don't," Barrow said, "and neither does George here, or Quinn, who owns the hotel."

"Care to tell me why?"

"I don't like his methods," Barrow said, and left it at that.

Garvin, however, went on. "We were grooming Victor here to represent this state at the capital—"

"George—" Barrow said.

"Oh, I get it," Clint said. "You're worried that Titus might get there ahead of you."

"Or instead," Scarlet added.

"Never mind that," Barrow said. "You said you knew a way to bring him down."

"I do."

"Tell us."

Clint did. It occurred to him on the spur of the moment, but the more he talked the more he felt it would work.

So did Barrow, who said, "All right, I know how to get the word passed to Titus, but then what?"

"Then you leave it to me," Scarlet said.

"To you?" Barrow asked, frowning. "I don't mean you any disrespect, ma'am, but I'd feel a lot better about this if you told me to let the Gunsmith here handle it."

Clint let the fact that Barrow knew who he was pass without comment. "Don't worry about Scarlet," he said. "She's got more against Titus than any of you."

"And you?"

"I hardly know the man."

Barrow looked at Scarlet with a puzzled expression and asked, "What have you got to do with Titus?"

"I'm going to kill him."

Barrow exchanged glances with Garvin, then said, "I can't go along with murder, even if it is John Titus."

"It'll be a fair fight," Scarlet said.

Barrow looked at Garvin again, then grabbed the brandy decanter from the desk, poured himself another drink, and said, "Well, then, that's different."

●　　●　　●

And so the word was passed, starting with a rumor from the bank teller; passed to a friend in the saloon, then to a friend of the friend, on and on until it reached the ears of someone who passed it on to Sheriff Resnick. From there it was only a matter of time until it reached Valin, and then John Titus.

"He's what?" Titus asked, not sure he had heard his foreman right.

"He's talking about pulling out. Went into the bank to see what kind of price he could get for his spread."

"He's trying to get the bank to buy him out because he knows I'm the only one around with enough money to do it," Titus said, rubbing his hands together.

"From what I hear, the bank isn't interested."

"Which means if he wants to get out, he's going to have to sell to me."

"Yes, sir."

"Once I've got Barrow's spread, nobody'll be able to stop me," Titus said with a faraway look in his eye.

"Except the girl."

Titus snapped a look at Valin, then nodded in agreement. "Yes, the girl is the problem," he admitted, "the only major problem now that Victor Barrow appears to be ready to pull out."

"How can you be sure, sir?" Valin asked. "This is just a rumor."

"There's only one way to be sure," Titus said, standing up behind his desk. Valin waited patiently while his boss did some fast thinking. "Saddle my horse," he said finally.

"Sir?"

"I'm going into town."

"Alone?"

"Of course not alone," Titus said, regarding Valin as he would a child who has failed a test. "I want you and some handpicked men to come with me."

"What are we going to do in town?"

"I'm going to talk with George Garvin at the bank and find out just how true this rumor is," Titus explained, "and then I want to talk with Bowman. He's going to have to do his job as quickly as possible. You and your men are going to make sure that girl doesn't get near me until he can kill her."

"I don't know if this is the right thing to do, Mr. Titus—"

"Don't worry about that, Valin," Titus said. "I'll decide what's right or wrong, okay?"

"Sure, Boss," Valin said doubtfully, "sure."

Valin left to take care of the details and Titus nervously paced his office, aware that much was within his grasp now. He walked to a chest against the far wall of the room and opened it. Inside was a flintlock, beautifully inlaid with silver. It came from his past. All he had to do was take care of the girl from his past.

From his past . . . and Bowman's past.

THIRTY-TWO

Scarlet, looking out the window of Clint's room, asked, "Do you think this is going to work?"

"A rumor like that?" he asked. "That Titus's main competition is pulling out? Our friend Titus won't be able to resist checking that out with Garvin."

"I hope you're right," she said, looking at him. "I appreciate you coming up with this idea, Clint, whether it works or not."

"There's only one thing I regret."

"What's that?"

"Barrow will benefit from this, as well," he said. "I don't think I like him any better than Titus."

"I don't want to sound like I'm getting nervous or anything," Scarlet said, scanning the main street again. "More like impatient. Titus is proving the most difficult so far. With the others all I had to do was call them out."

"Give it a chance, Scarlet," Clint said. "Even if it doesn't work, we'll think of something else, but if I was you I wouldn't stand by the window."

"Why not?"

"With that red hair," he told her, "you make a hell of a target."

"Look," she said, staring intently out the window.

He got up off the bed where he had been reclining and joined her by the window.

Together they watched as John Titus, his foreman Valin, and four other men rode into town. They rode to the bank, where Titus dismounted and went inside with Valin. The other four men remained outside.

"It worked," Scarlet said.

"That's it," Clint said. "Let's go."

Others had also noticed the Titus crew's procession down the main street.

Sheriff Resnick watched from his office window, nervously wondering if a fuse was about to be lit beneath his nice quiet town.

Danny O'Shay watched from his hiding place—the roof of the general store across the street. He had been hiding out until he could come up with a way of drawing the red-haired woman out and away from the Gunsmith. Seeing Titus and Valin in town told him that something big was about to happen. He scrambled down from the roof to join the fray.

Ross Bowman could not see John Titus because he was in the boardinghouse at the other end of town. He had other eyes, however, and when Phyllis Gibson came out of the general store and saw Titus enter the bank, she knew that Bowman would want to know.

Clint had ascertained earlier that the hotel had a rear exit. In fact, it had been shown to him by Quinn, the hotel owner, to whom the situation had been explained by the other two, Barrow and Garvin. As far as Clint knew, all that Quinn had against Titus was that he, too, was a Barrow supporter.

Politics, he thought. It had never been an area of interest for him—in fact, it was an area of disinterest.

Clint and Scarlet left the hotel by the rear exit and made their way to the rear of the bank, where there was a door that opened directly into George Garvin's office. They pressed their ears against the door and were able to hear voices and make out what they were saying.

"All I'm doing is checking on a rumor, George," John Titus said.

"What sort of rumor is that, Titus?" the bank president asked.

"I heard something about Victor Barrow looking for a buyer for his ranch," Titus said. "I also heard that he offered it to the bank and that you had no interest. If the rumor is true, then I *am* interested."

"Well, Titus," Garvin said, a smile almost creasing his lined face, "the rumor is not true."

"What?"

"That's our cue," Clint said, and opened the door George Garvin had left unlocked. As he stepped into the room, John Titus stopped talking in midsentence and stared.

"Adams," he said after a few moments.

"Hello, Titus—don't make a move for that gun, Valin," he warned as he read the look on the foreman's face. "Not unless you're feeling real lucky."

Titus looked at Valin and said, "Relax, Frank. We came here to talk." Looking first at Clint and then at Garvin, he said, "I don't understand what's going on here. I heard a rumor—"

"A rumor started by me," Clint said.

"By you?" Titus asked, narrowing his eyes. He gave Garvin a puzzled look, then directed himself to the Gunsmith and demanded, "Why?"

"I was helping out a friend."

"A friend," Titus said. "Look, I don't appreciate being the butt of some joke—"

"No joke," Scarlet said, stepping into the room.

"You!"

"It's been a long time, Mr. Tillman," Scarlet said, pulling the door shut behind her. "Mr. James Tillman."

THIRTY-THREE

"Tillman?" Garvin asked, taking his turn at looking puzzled now.

"Yes," Scarlet said. "That was his name five years ago, when he murdered my entire family and tried to murder me."

Garvin's mouth dropped open and he stared at the man he knew as John Titus, as if he were seeing him for the first time.

"I could sue you, young lady," Titus said.

"I could kill *you*, James Tillman."

A muscle jumped in Titus/Tillman's jaw. "My name is Titus, John Titus," he said, "and I've never met you before in my life."

He turned to leave, but Scarlet's biting tone stopped him before he could reach the door. "Actually, we never were properly introduced, that's true, Tillman," Scarlet said, "but we were on very intimate terms, weren't we?"

Titus turned and stared at Scarlet. "Miss—"

"Let's stop the games, Tillman," Clint said. "It's all over anyway. Your new life is shattered."

173

"My *new* life—"

"I think you'd better start worrying about your old one."

"I don't understand why I was lured here," Titus said, attempting to affect impatience.

"So that you and I could finish our business, Tillman," Scarlet answered, "business that started five years ago."

"What is she talking about, Mr. Titus?" Valin asked.

"Shut up!" Titus/Tillman snapped. "Don't listen to her—"

"Your boss and four other men killed my family after raping my younger sister and me. They thought I was dead, but I'm not—and now two of them are. Tillman will follow them very soon."

"Rape?" Valin said, staring at Titus. Frank Valin would do a lot of things that were perhaps not strictly within the letter of the law, but rape was alien to him. It would never occur to him to rape a woman, especially a young woman. This one couldn't have been more than seventeen five years ago, and she claimed that her *younger* sister had also been attacked.

"Valin, go outside and get the men—"

"Stay where you are, Valin," Clint said.

"Don't worry, Adams," Valin said, still staring at Titus. "If what this lady says is true—"

"Of course it's not true!"

"Then tell your foreman why you're so afraid of this young woman," Garvin said, jumping into the conversation.

"Yes," Valin said, "why?"

Titus looked around the room at the other four

people and did not see one friendly face.

"What—what do you want?" he asked Scarlet.

"I want to kill you."

Titus rubbed his hand over his dry lips, then looked at the other men.

"You can't," he said anxiously, "you can't just let her gun me down!"

"We don't intend to," Clint said. "It will be fair. You're wearing a gun."

Titus jumped back and stared at the gun on his hip as if it would bite him any minute. "I'm no gunman!"

"Valin," Clint said, "you can leave. Go back to the ranch and take the others with you."

Valin nodded and looked at Titus.

"Don't think about waiting outside for us," Clint warned him. "My first bullet will find you."

"Don't worry," Valin said. "I'm going back to the ranch."

Valin left the room, rounded the cage area, and strode to the front of the bank. Looking out the window he saw that this could all be to his benefit. After all, what would happen to Titus—or Tillman's—property after he was dead? Valin wondered, with the money he'd been putting away, how much of it he could pick up cheap at auction?

"What's happening?" Moss asked as Valin stepped outside.

"Mount up," he said. "We're going back."

"All right, Mr. Tillman," Clint said, "let's go."

"W-where?"

"Outside."

The man's eyes darted toward the front door nervously, and Clint said, "No, not that way. The way we came in. Just in case a few of your men are hanging around."

"Garvin, you can't let this happen—"

"Tillman, Victor and I checked out this young lady's story as completely as we could. We sent telegrams and received replies. We know that a family was killed, just as she says. We believe enough of her story to believe the rest of it—that you owe her something."

"Something that can only be repaid out on the street, Tillman," Scarlet said. "Let's go."

Bowman was walking toward the bank as Valin and the other men passed him. He turned to watch them ride out of town and knew that something was wrong. They'd left Titus alone and that would never have been Titus's own idea.

The bank. Phyllis had said that Titus had gone into the bank.

Bowman stormed into the bank and looked around, ignoring the teller's attempts to find out if they could help him. Spotting the door marked PRESIDENT, he rounded the cage and, as the young teller tried to step in front of him, viciously backhanded the man out of his way.

He slammed the door open and regarded the frightened man behind the desk.

"A-are you robbing the bank?" Garvin stammered.

"I have one question," Bowman said tersely, "and if you answer it, you might live past the next few seconds."

THIRTY-FOUR

The plan was to take Tillman behind the livery stable, where he would face-off with Scarlet.

They walked with Scarlet in front of Tillman and Clint Adams behind, and Tillman wondered six different times during the five-minute walk whether he'd be able to draw his gun and shoot the woman in the back before Adams could shoot *him*. Six different times he decided that he couldn't.

An equal amount of times he tried to talk the two of them out of it, calling it madness, telling Scarlet that she had made a mistake, but just as many times they'd ignored him.

Bowman, damn it, where the hell are you when I need you? he shouted mentally.

"All right," Clint said as they reached their destination. "Walk to the other end of this corral, Tillman."

"I want to know something first."

"What?"

"If I kill her," he said, "will you kill me?"

"No," Scarlet said, answering before Clint could.

"If you kill me in a fair fight then that's it, you and the two after you all win."

Tillman looked at Adams for confirmation and the Gunsmith said, "That's the way the lady wants it."

Tillman saw a glimmer of hope in this as he walked to the far end of the corral. He wasn't a gunman, that was true, but she was, after all, just a woman.

"That's far enough," Clint called.

Tillman stopped.

"Still want to go through with this?" Clint asked Scarlet.

"Of course."

"No second thoughts?"

"None."

Clint was sorry to hear that, but he understood her thirst for vengeance. He had felt it himself—possibly to the same degree—on two different occasions. The first was when he heard that his friend Hickok had been murdered,* and the second was when a woman he loved, Joanna Morgan, took a bullet meant for him and died.†

"All right," Clint called out. "Whenever you're ready."

As Clint Adams shouted this out, Tillman looked past him and saw, just inside the livery, Ross Bowman. Relief washed over him. He looked at Scarlet then, sure that just as she drew, Bowman would cut her down. After that, it would be Bowman and Adams, and if Tillman could, he'd shoot Adams in the back.

All right, bitch, he thought, come and get it.

Ross Bowman was standing behind Clint Adams and

---

*The Gunsmith #14: Dead Man's Hand.
†The Gunsmith #25: North of the Border.

Scarlet. For a brief moment his eyes met those of James Tillman.

Good luck, he thought.

He'd never liked Tillman anyway.

Tillman made an honest attempt at outdrawing Scarlet because, feeling safe with Bowman there, the attempt amused him.

She was very fast, he thought, as she clearly outdrew him. He looked past her, saw Bowman watching, and during the split second before he died realized that the gunman was going to do nothing to help him.

"No!" he shouted just before the bullet struck him on the left side of the chest, driving him back against the corral fence.

He fell facedown in the dirt, but didn't know it.

Clint was about to walk toward the fallen man when he heard something behind him that made him stop.

Applause.

Both he and Scarlet turned and saw Ross Bowman coming out of the livery stable, applauding.

"Very nicely done, ma'am," Bowman said. He stopped applauding them and dropped his hands to his side. "Now let's see if the Gunsmith can do as well with me."

"The Gunsmith?" Scarlet asked. "I thought you were here for me, Mr.—your name is Bowman, isn't it?"

"That's right."

"You look like someone . . . " she said, frowning.

"I did come here for you originally, Miss . . . Scarlet? Yes, but that was before I knew that Clint Adams was here."

With that Bowman looked at Clint and said, "You know this is inevitable. You've known it since that night in the saloon, haven't you?"

Clint sighed and said, "Yes, Bowman. It's always inevitable."

"If you're not happy with your rep, Adams, I'll be glad to take it off your hands."

"Clint—" Scarlet started.

"Move aside, Scarlet," he said. "We'll talk later."

"Oh, very confidently said," Bowman said admiringly, "but you better kiss your ladyfriend now, Adams, because there isn't going to be a later."

"Get it over with, Bowman," Clint said. "I've got things to do."

"At the top of your list," Bowman said, "write *die.*"

Bowman went for his gun and Scarlet, her eyes on him, had never seen a faster move in her life. She heard the shot but did not see Bowman's gun buck. A dot of red blossomed on Bowman's chest, on the left side, and he staggered back, dropped his gun, opened his mouth as if to speak . . . and died.

Clint checked James Tillman and found that, like Ross Bowman, he was dead. He walked back to where Scarlet was standing, looking down at Ross Bowman.

She looked up at Clint as he reached her and said, "He was fast."

"Yes," Clint agreed, "he was."

"I didn't see you—"

"You were looking at him," Clint pointed out.

"You saw me—"

"I saw everything, Scarlet," he said. "If you don't, you'll end up dead."

"She may end up dead anyway," a voice called from behind them.

Clint closed his eyes and thought—not again.

They both turned to face Danny O'Shay.

"Shit, Danny—" Clint said.

"Got yourself a student you like better than me, Clint?" he asked.

"I don't need a teacher," Scarlet said. "Who are you?"

"I'm the man who's going to kill you."

"Danny—"

"Stay out of this, Clint."

"You know him?"

"He's the main reason I'm here," Clint said. "I came to keep him from doing something foolish—like this."

"Clint, shall I—"

"Come on, Clint," Danny O'Shay shouted, "wait your turn."

"You young idiot!" Clint snapped. "Your sister asked me to find you, Danny. Think of what you're doing to Sheena."

"I'm through talking," he said. "I'll draw on either one of you."

"Danny don't—"

O'Shay's hand moved for his gun and to Clint it seemed that he was moving in slow motion. He drew his own gun and fired one shot.

Scarlet couldn't believe it. Again, she'd been watching the wrong man, but this time she was glad. She heard the shot and saw the holster fly from the young man's hip before he could reach his gun.

"You shot the holster off his hip," she said, staring at Clint.

"I didn't want to kill him," Clint said, holstering his gun and walking to where Danny O'Shay stood, stunned and in shock.

"Y-you shot the holster—"

"I could have shot off all of your buttons before you reached your gun, you young fool."

"You told me you didn't do trick shooting."

"The trick here," Clint said, "was in saving your life."

THIRTY-FIVE

They went into the livery and saddled three horses: Duke, Scarlet's bay, and the dun Danny O'Shay had ridden into town.

They rode first to the hotel, where Scarlet stayed outside with Danny while Clint went in, collected their things, and settled both their hotel bills.

Outside, he handed Scarlet her saddlebags and rifle and she asked, "Where are you going now?"

"To the sheriff's office."

They rode down to the lawman's office and he stepped out to meet them.

"I heard shots," he said. "Is it over?"

"It's over, Sheriff," Clint said. "You'll find Titus and Bowman over behind the livery. Looks to me like they shot each other."

"Titus shot Bowman?"

"And Bowman shot Titus."

"You expect anybody to believe that?"

Clint shrugged and said, "Can't say I really care, Sheriff."

They rode to the far end of town, past the boarding-house where a weary Phyllis Gibson was packing her bags to leave town on the next stage, whether Bowman came back or not.

Outside of town they stopped, Clint and Scarlet looking at each other, Danny O'Shay sitting silently between them.

"Where are you off to?" she asked.

"I have to take Danny back to his sister and then see if there's any law looking for him."

"Can you help him?"

Clint shrugged and said, "I hope I already have."

She nodded.

"What about you?"

"Well, I can ride a ways with you, if you don't mind," she said, "but then we'll have to split up."

"That's right," he said. "You've still got that fourth and fifth man to find."

She shook her head and said, "Just the fifth."

Clint frowned and said, "I don't understand."

"Bowman," she said.

"What about him?"

"When he came out of the livery stable it was the first clear look I had at him," she said. "It took me a few moments, but I placed him."

"You mean—"

"His name was Booth then," she said, "and he looked a little different, but he was the fourth man."

"Which means it's four down. . . ."

"Yes," she said, "and one to go. . . ."

J. R. ROBERTS

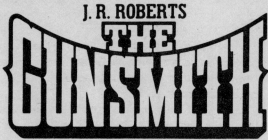

THE GUNSMITH

SERIES

☐ 30925-9	THE GUNSMITH	#5:	THREE GUNS FOR GLORY	$2.50
☐ 30861-9	THE GUNSMITH	#6:	LEADTOWN	$2.25
☐ 30862-7	THE GUNSMITH	#7:	THE LONGHORN WAR	$2.25
☐ 30901-1	THE GUNSMITH	#8:	QUANAH'S REVENGE	$2.50
☐ 30923-2	THE GUNSMITH	#9:	HEAVYWEIGHT GUN	$2.50
☐ 30924-0	THE GUNSMITH	#10:	NEW ORLEANS FIRE	$2.50
☐ 30931-3	THE GUNSMITH	#11:	ONE-HANDED GUN	$2.50
☐ 30926-7	THE GUNSMITH	#12:	THE CANADIAN PAYROLL	$2.50
☐ 30927-5	THE GUNSMITH	#13:	DRAW TO AN INSIDE DEATH	$2.50
☐ 30922-4	THE GUNSMITH	#14:	DEAD MAN'S HAND	$2.50
☐ 30905-4	THE GUNSMITH	#15:	BANDIT GOLD	$2.50
☐ 30886-4	THE GUNSMITH	#16:	BUCKSKINS AND SIX-GUNS	$2.25
☐ 30887-2	THE GUNSMITH	#17:	SILVER WAR	$2.25
☐ 30908-9	THE GUNSMITH	#18:	HIGH NOON AT LANCASTER	$2.50
☐ 30909-7	THE GUNSMITH	#19:	BANDIDO BLOOD	$2.50
☐ 30929-1	THE GUNSMITH	#20:	THE DODGE CITY GANG	$2.50
☐ 30910-0	THE GUNSMITH	#21:	SASQUATCH HUNT	$2.50
☐ 30894-5	THE GUNSMITH	#23:	THE RIVERBOAT GANG	$2.25
☐ 30895-3	THE GUNSMITH	#24:	KILLER GRIZZLY	$2.50

Prices may be slightly higher in Canada.

Available at your local bookstore or return this form to:

CHARTER BOOKS
Book Mailing Service
P.O. Box 690, Rockville Centre, NY 11571

Please send me the titles checked above. I enclose _____. Include 75¢ for postage and handling if one book is ordered; 25¢ per book for two or more not to exceed $1.75. California, Illinois, New York and Tennessee residents please add sales tax.

NAME _____

ADDRESS _____

CITY _____ STATE/ZIP _____

(allow six weeks for delivery.)   A1

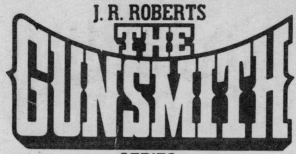

J. R. ROBERTS
THE GUNSMITH

SERIES

J.D. HARDIN

"THE MOST EXCITING WESTERN WRITER SINCE LOUIS L'AMOUR"
—JAKE LOGAN

____	872-16869-7	THE SPIRIT AND THE FLESH	$1.95
____	867-21226-8	BOBBIES, BAUBLES AND BLOOD	$2.25
____	06572-3	DEATH LODE	$2.25
____	06380-1	THE FIREBRANDS	$2.25
____	06410-7	DOWNRIVER TO HELL	$2.25
____	06001-2	BIBLES, BULLETS AND BRIDES	$2.25
____	06331-3	BLOODY TIME IN BLACKTOWER	$2.25
____	06248-1	HANGMAN'S NOOSE	$2.25
____	06337-2	THE MAN WITH NO FACE	$2.25
____	06151-5	SASKATCHEWAN RISING	$2.25
____	06412-3	BOUNTY HUNTER	$2.50
____	06743-2	QUEENS OVER DEUCES	$2.50
____	07017-4	LEAD-LINED COFFINS	$2.50
____	08013-7	THE WYOMING SPECIAL	$2.50
____	07259-2	THE PECOS DOLLARS	$2.50
____	07257-6	SAN JUAN SHOOTOUT	$2.50
____	07379-3	OUTLAW TRAIL	$2.50
____	07392-0	THE OZARK OUTLAWS	$2.50
____	07461-7	TOMBSTONE IN DEADWOOD	$2.50
____	07381-5	HOMESTEADER'S REVENGE	$2.50
____	07386-6	COLORADO SILVER QUEEN	$2.50
____	07790-X	THE BUFFALO SOLDIER	$2.50
____	07785-3	THE GREAT JEWEL ROBBERY	$2.50
____	07789-6	THE COCHISE COUNTY WAR	$2.50
____	07684-9	APACHE TRAIL	$2.50
____	07754-3	IN THE HEART OF TEXAS	$2.50
____	07974-0	THE COLORADO STING	$2.50
____	08032-3	HELL'S BELLE	$2.50

Prices may be slightly higher in Canada.